CW01084709

Game of Gnomes:
The Necrognomicon

By

M. J. Northwood

Published by
Critical Tales

Front cover image & book design by Carrie Copa
Edited by Antony Titley and Isobel Meally

Copyright © M. J. Northwood 2020

All rights reserved. No part of this publication
may be reproduced or transmitted in any form or by
any means, electronic or mechanical, including photocopy,
recording, or any information storage and retrieval system,
without permission in writing from the copyright owner.

Website: www.criticaltales.co.uk
Email: info@criticaltales.co.uk
Facebook: @criticaltalesofficial

For all other enquires please use
info@criticaltales.co.uk

Chapter One

Bang... and other such alarming onomatopoeias had been berating Gassy Bedchambers' ears for several hours now. The unfortunately-named, plump little gnome was lucky enough to have a sturdy shelter from the increasingly persistent storm outside. At least, that's what he would lead any lost, weary travellers to believe. Not that he'd seen any. In fact, he'd chosen this place for its dangerous isolation.

When perusing for this precariously placed tower, Gassy's first impression was how wonderfully awkward the journey was. From the nearest major town, you would need four separate horse-and-cart rides, three shoddily maintained rowboats, two slow (and surprisingly chatty) ooze-ogres, and one unpredictable and nippy giant vulture. Well, I suppose you could skip everything else and just go straight for the giant vulture, but only a maniac with a death wish would make that journey.

No, Gassy was quite certain he had found the world's most secluded studio wizard's tower. A purchase he'd made with a fortune that was 'definitely legitimately earned and not at all gained from criminal activity', as he repeatedly said to the estate agent.

Yes, he was absolutely alone. He was sheltered from the outside world. Just him, his work, his equally sheltered vegetable garden, and his extensive collection of rare erotic novels. Not a soul nearby.

"Hello?" said a nearby soul through the door, followed by a rather commanding knock.

"Umm...hello?" Gassy responded with unreasonably intense verbosity. His first discussion with a disembodied voice for quite some time and he thought it was going rather well, so far.

"Gassy?" queried the voice.

Golly, thought Gassy, this voice already knows my name. I'm better at conversation than I remember.

"Gassy. Let me in. I've come a long way."

Well, there wasn't much point arguing with the muffled voice behind the door. Although he wasn't quite as presentable as he would like, Gassy walked over to his home's heavily reinforced entrance and unlocked the extensive series of locks. Behind the door was a familiar face.

"Borty Beetle-bowel! How in the gods' names did you get here?" said Gassy.

"That's a very good question," replied Borty.

"Oh, thank you very much," beamed Gassy.

"You're most welcome." Borty strode into the abode as far as his short, gnomey legs would take him. "Gassy, I need you."

"Oh my. That's very forward of you and it is definitely tempting—"

"I need you to help me with a new heist I'm planning," continued Borty.

"Ah...Of course. Just hand over the building plans and I'll find you a way in," said Gassy as he trundled over to his writing desk.

"No, Gassy! That's no use to me. I need you. Crimicon is back on." Borty trounced over to Gassy and grabbed him by the shoulders. "The Crimicompetition is back on."

"No, no, and no again. There's no way I'm going back there after what happened last time. There's a reason they closed the doors on that convention." Gassy slipped out of Borty's grasp and hurried over to the comfort of his vast book collection.

"Don't be so melodramatic, Gassy. What's a Crimicon without a few deaths?"

The 'few deaths' Borty was referring to was actually somewhat closer to a 'little massacre'. The Crimicon would bring in tens of thousands of criminals annually with a new exciting theme each year. One of Gassy's favourites was the ladder theme. Being a fan of everything taller than him – which was most things – Gassy adored walking around the convention, seeing the creative ways ladders were put to good use. Ladder-based shoes, ladders made of horses, horses made of ladders, even a ladder designed to go down as well as up. *What marvellous creations*, he'd think to himself. But not on that fateful day. Not on the day of 'Crimicon: Bottled Crime'.

It might sound perfectly harmless to you. 'Oh. What danger is crime if it's in a bottle?', well the answer is clear. Very dangerous. In fact, it's so dangerous that exactly four-hundred-and-seventy-nine lives were lost according to statistics reported in a review of the event from The Rolling Gnomes magazine. The same review also went on a lengthy tangent about the origins of bottles and what a difficult childhood bottles had, so you make your own judgement on its credibility. Still, 'Whatever happened?' you may ask, 'for such a scathing report of the event,' you may continue. Well, it was an act of crime against criminals. Something so dastardly that even the sturdiest of the underworld daren't speak of it. Something so awful that only the greatest, most talented of authors could put to words the sheer agony of the crime. Unfortunately for you, this author is a bumbling buffoon with more hairs on his arse then words in his head, so instead we'll just get back to the story.

"You're calling me melodramatic?! I nearly died, Borty!" gassed Gassy, "I haven't used a bottle since! Do you realise how inconvenient it is storing honey in a paper bag?"

"A paper bag? Why not just use a jar?"

"Because some chirpy, strangely sexy bear kept sneaking into my house and eating my honey right out the jar." Gassy was shuffling papers around with unreasonable force. "The only way to keep it out was to use a bag."

"That makes a lot of sense. You did buy a place in a rough area as far as bears go." Borty quickly realised their digression and brought the conversation back to the matter at hand. "Listen, yes, we all nearly died. Lots of people nearly die every day, you don't hear them complaining."

"I don't hear much of anything from anyone these days."

"Exactly! It's about time you got out for a bit," Borty argued. "If I'm being honest, I need this. It's not been easy working jobs without you. I need this win, Gassy." Borty's silver tongue and extra two inches of height were too difficult for Gassy to argue against. How could he protest against such a magnificent gnome?

"But why me, Borty? There are plenty of other gnomes out there with the same set of skills."

"Because I'm putting together a team. A small team. A really small team. A team I can trust. And I trust you."

Gassy squeezed out a cautious smile. "I'm not sure I'm ready."

"Gassy, it's been years. We've all had bad heists before. There's no better way to get past yours than to take on the biggest heist of the year."

"You mean Crimicon. What was this year's theme again?"

Borty also smiled. He had already hooked Gassy, and he knew it. "Crimicon: Four Feet Under."

"Four Feet Under? That's not the saying. Surely you mean six," said Gassy.

"No, it's definitely four. I'm certain of it." Borty didn't even blink.

"Right..." said Gassy with a fraction of a frown, "fine. You know I can't say no to you," Gassy submitted, completely unaware of just how correct he was. In actuality, not once has Gassy turned down a request for help from Borty. He has tried, sure, but his resistance has never really lasted. This wasn't exclusive to Gassy either. Most people Borty interacted with had trouble disappointing him. Any time he has ever asked for something, *really* asked for it, he's gotten it. The satisfaction of Borty's desires have even manifested in some truly bizarre ways. Unfortunately, this innate talent for persuasion has remained unknown to any living thing. Not even Borty is aware. Even more regrettably, this remarkable power continues to be largely unused due to Borty's can-do attitude. He's only ever asked for ten things in his life and three of those things were requests for songs on GGC's Radio Gnome.

Gassy hurried over to the edges of his study and picked up a prepacked, travel-sized backpack that could easily be carried as a handbag. It overflowed with only a few books and a couple of other trinkets. Once he slipped-on his booties and gave a few of his potted plants a farewell kiss (no tongues of course, not in front of guests), Gassy rushed over to Borty.

"Were you already packed?" Borty asked.

Hesitantly, Gassy responded, "Yes. It's just in case, y'know." Gassy adjusted his overcoat and struggled to look Borty in the eye.

"In case of what?"

"Ohh, y'know... in case I need to leave in a rush." Gassy shuffled on the spot. "Anyway, we should hurry. We don't want to miss the giant vulture."

"The what?" Borty opened the door into the raging storm, squinting as the rain hit the side of his face.

"The thing you flew here on. It's the only public transport onto this—" before he could finish that thought, Gassy was distracted by the most stunning beauty he had ever laid eyes on. A bouncing brunette with long dripping-wet locks draping across her carefully curving neck. Luscious lashes flicked with anticipation as her enormous brown eyes locked with his. Gassy's presence was graced by her powerful thighs that seemed to go all the way up to her bountiful chest. A tight leather bodice just barely held her bulging bosom in place, but did nothing to hide her bodacious booty. He could see her bottom from the front, so he knew it would be a treat from behind. It was the most beautiful ass he'd ever seen.

"She's the most beautiful woman I've ever seen."

"Woman? That's a donkey."

Gassy's eyes widened. He inspected the 'donkey' with great attention. He then keeled over himself as he realised the beauty in front of him was indeed a donkey. Not a rude description of an aesthetically unappealing person, but an actual donkey.

You see, much to Gassy's dismay, his extended period in solitude with his many erotic novels had changed his perception of women. Who would have thought it? After such a long time apart from women, he had begun to perceive them based on the overt objectifications of other hermits who had equally limited experience with the opposing gender. It may seem somewhat silly, but you'd be surprised at the amount of nonsense people are willing to accept into their reality with the right amount of miseducation.

"Enough smoodging around. Hop on the donkey and we'll be off," suggested Borty.

"Yeah. Okay." Gassy's posture instantly changed into a slink. Where his intellect had once been a source of pride, he was suddenly reminded of its limits. He at least found comfort in the thought that the donkey was indeed quite the looker, as far as donkeys go.

In a bit of a strop, Gassy clumsily straddled the donkey. Far more gracefully, Borty settled in behind Gassy in the spacious saddle.

"Mind your legs. Make some room for the wings," said Borty. Gassy complied before getting caught on his words.

"Wait, wings?"

Yes, wings. A fact that taunted Gassy for years to come as they stretched out in front of him like a branch being pulled through tar.

"What's wrong now?" sighed Borty.

Unsure how to react, Gassy gawked. "Why does it have wings?"

"It's a donkey. All donkeys have wings," said Borty, incorrectly. For those unfamiliar with donkeys, they most certainly don't have wings. This was something Gassy was absolutely certain about, but could he trust anything he believed anymore? *Best not to question it*, he thought, only to be immediately betrayed by his mouth.

"The wings are sticky too! Why are they sticky?"

"Are you seriously still talking about the donkey? Listen, I don't want to hear another bad word about it for the whole ride. The donkey doesn't like it." Borty's last few words really put the fear of the gods into Gassy. *Did the donkey understand me?* The question kept him quiet during take-off. And a rather shaky take-off it was. Once they left the immediate shelter of Gassy's porchway, grumbling gales and raindrops as big as fingernails crashed into them from all sides. Yet the donkey powered through. Even with the extra weight, this typically flightless farm animal found itself comfortably airborne in seconds.

Before long, Gassy watched his luxurious tower disappear behind thick, low-lying rainclouds as they breached the calm of the upper layer.

"Now it's just a straight flight to town."

"Where are we going?"

"To see an old friend. Stay wrapped-up, it's going to get pretty chilly!" yelled Borty. And chilly it most certainly did get.

Chapter Two

Soaring over the wild watery hills of Abbitmorre was a unique experience for Gassy. Most time spent with Borty usually resulted in unique experiences.

Abbitmorre was a relatively small town compared to what the country had to offer, but what it lacked in size it made up for with interesting travellers. Its placement on one of the busiest intercity roads made for a flourishing settlement filled with curious individuals. At least, that's how it used to be. Only a few months ago the upper council finished work on a bypass through the swamplands saving commuters a valuable twenty minutes and only costing the leadership their road maintenance budget for the next five years. A fair trade in the eyes of the upper council.

"Hold tight!" Borty yelled as their admiration of the town was cut short by a hasty landing.

"Golly! What's the rush?" asked Gassy.

"Sorry. Down-on-their-luck townsfolk around here have started to shoot at anything they see in the sky for an easy meal. Best not to risk it." Borty majestically guided the donkey to the ground. They settled outside an old barn.

"What's the plan then? Who's this old friend we're meeting?" Gassy ungracefully slid from his seat atop the donkey onto the muddy ground. Well, he certainly hoped it was mud.

"You'll see. But he's the only one we need. With the three of us together, we're guaranteed to win this year's Crimicompetition." Borty's dismount was significantly more impressive. The moment they had unpacked everything from the back of the donkey, it took to the air.

"Woah, woah, woah! Borty, the donkey, it's... flying away." Gassy still found the unusual beast hard to come to terms with, even after a couple hours of flight.

"Gassy, I'm going to say this in the nicest way possible. I think you have a problem. You seem obsessed with that donkey. Why do you keep bringing it up? It's weird. Honestly, when this is all said and done, I think you should get some help." Borty's subtle disgust was enough to shut Gassy up.

* * * * *

Abbitmorre was quiet. The pair had been meandering through the buildings for almost a half-hour now and they'd hardly seen more than a dozen people. Even as they approached the only paved road in the town, barely a handful of faces could be spotted.

"This is bad for us," wheezed Gassy. Sweat dribbled down his poorly-shaved chin after such a long walk.

"I know. There's no crowd to blend into," said Borty as he peered from the corner of a shoddily maintained building, "anyone sees the two of us lurking around and they'll assume the worst."

Quite rightfully too. Although steeped in prejudice and blatant racism, the common stereotype that gnomes were all thieves was almost entirely true. You could go so far as to say it was a fact were it not for the few gnomes that upgraded to murder and one unusual gnome that found his calling in 'The Nunnery of Nothing', a rather well-received stage play about the day-to-day lives of a group of nuns whose god died, where this particular gnome found his role as the head nun's coronet.

"We need to split up then," said Gassy.

"Good idea. Hopefully, if the townsfolk see us, they'll just assume we're the same person," said Borty.

"We should prepare a careful search plan so we don't cross paths."

"We don't need to worry about it that much," said Borty.

"I'd prefer to put together a strateg—"

"I'll head to the pubs," said Borty, "you go to the market. Chances are, he's probably pissed someone off already."

"I really would prefer we think—" Before Gassy could finish his sentence, Borty had scarpered.

I don't even know who I'm looking for, Gassy thought to himself. Still, the only plan he had was to search the marketplace, so that's where he'd start. Even if it was a weak plan.

In only a few minutes, he'd already found the market in the town square. He stood on the precipice of this wonderfully ornate square with weathered marble sculptures and fading regal tapestries hanging from carefully carved entablatures. The perfectly spaced colonnades around the square were a far more impressive build than the rest of the town had to offer. It was all so beautiful. It was also... empty. Not a single person in sight.

At first, Gassy had assumed the new bypass had hit the town harder than expected. It *was* a trading town after all. Then, he noticed the stalls. Densely-packed and moderately stocked market stalls were set up all across the square. Half-filled with fruit, veggies, herbs, spices, and even a few potions.

"Who would leave all this lovely, stealable, stuff?" Gassy asked himself aloud. There was even an abandoned beggar's sign that read: 'Pleez Giv Muney'. How could any self-respecting gnome pass-up an opportunity this delicious? As his sticky hands reached for the shiniest thing nearby, he was interrupted.

Gong, chimed a big gong. *Gong*. A second time. It was coming from the clock tower of a nearby repurposed abbey. *Gong*, it struck for the third and final time. *Hold on, that clock is definitely wrong*, thought Gassy. The town's clock tower was indeed on the fritz. So, to keep track of time, they hired a hunchback to hit a big gong on the important hours. Unbeknownst to the rest of the town, Hughey the hunchback was hired without ever learning to tell the time so he just guessed: today's lunchtime, for example, had been especially long. Most people would have been fired a long time ago for incompetence as blatant as Hughey's, but what they lacked was Hughey's extraordinary talent for avoiding confrontation. At every hour (a Hughey hour, to be precise), Hughey carried the gong to a new location; a gong twice his size, mind you. After the third week of trying to find him, people just gave up and accepted it. It just so happened, that today, he was in the clock tower.

Gassy stood completely still. The chiming still echoing through the square. Suddenly, he spotted movement. A disappointed old man shuffled past parked carts and verandas. His grumblings could be heard all the way from where Gassy stood but were quickly replaced with more footsteps. A group this time, some chortling farmers stumbled their way back to their stalls. They were shortly followed by a handful of ladies. Ladies. Women. Gassy got stuck on that thought for a few moments. They were everything his books described only with slightly more colour to their cheeks, or with noses a touch wonkier and clothes significantly more practical.

"Don't get distracted," he yelled at himself, accompanying his words with a couple hardy slaps. With his mind focused on the goal, he discovered himself completely surrounded with streams of people. In an instant, the machine of the market seemed to be running again.

He started to dive between the many market stalls. His eyes were darting faster than his body could move. The sudden surge of people made it impossible to pick anyone out, especially from his vertically-challenged vantage point. He stopped and started. People shoved past him with drunken grumbles.

Gassy's pace quickened. His eyes did too. The hip-height world offered him no respite from his growing desperation. He was reaching for any chance to finish his task. A few floating faces filled him with excitement, only to quickly disappoint as he realised they were just people tying their shoelaces or picking up boxes.

Then he saw someone. They were far away, standing at the furthest edge of the market.

Was it a trick of the eye? Depth-of-field maybe? Each step he took increased his heart-rate as he realised this figure was indeed someone short. His walking evolved into a light jog. A very light jog. He 'weaved' through the legs of careless passers-by, all of whom dismissed Gassy as an obnoxious child. He approached the figure with unbridled glee, reaching out.

Five steps. Three steps. One step.

Gassy grabbed them by the hood, spun them around and placed his hands on their bare shoulder, just about ready to kiss them...then his face dropped.

The face looking back at him was not that of a gnome, but a hurgle. In its own right, the face of your average purebred hurgle isn't particularly horrifying unless you have a crippling fear of toads. No, its amphibious face wasn't what scared Gassy. It was what he knew about hurgles from his surprisingly detailed erotic novel collection. If there's anything Gassy learned from his erotica, it's a fairly accurate depiction of each race's reproductive process, if not a little overdramatised. His impressive knowledge of interspecies relations includes that of the hurgles.

A hurgle, unlike most species you might come across, is a hyper-adaptive-super-producer as categorised by the guide 'A List of Every Race and Where to Stick It', an independent piece which was promptly stolen and republished by MagInc who responded to public outcry with their company motto 'Don't Question Us'. The adaptive-super-producer category is shared by the Karanites who are famous for the highest rate of teen pregnancy in the known universe, mostly owed to the fact they would reproduce at the mere thought of the act regardless of who's 'participating'. Sex education classes quickly became parenting lessons in their curriculum.

"Bugger," squeezed out Gassy. He slowly began to retreat with fear.

"Bugga? Das all you 'ave t'say for yaself?" barked the increasingly displeased hurgle.

"I'm very sor—" Gassy began before he noticed a boil on the hurgle's neck begin to swell.

"Sorry ain't gunna cuh it mista. Ya behha take responsibili'y for dis." The hurgle's already strong accent was becoming harder to understand as its neck-growth expanded exponentially. It took everything Gassy had to keep him from gagging in front of this revolting display, an action that would be considered the height of bad manners.

"Is there..." Gassy paused. His train of thought was distracted as the light silhouetted the contents of the neck node. Inside, was a baby. "Umm...is there anything I can do to help?"

"Help? Ya made dis mess... is yours now," the hurgle was struggling to stand at this point as the weight of its new creation weighed down its head.

After just about grasping what the hurgle was trying to say, Gassy responded with a responsible choice.

"Very well. I'll take care of it," he professed. An agreement he'd quickly come to regret.

Watching over the hurgle's gestation was just the beginning. Gassy stood by as he watched the hurgle grow this tumour to half the size of its body before the sack detached.

"Break it," the hurgle commanded.

Obeying its wishes, Gassy tore open a small hole in the tough, gooey outer layer. Inside, he could see some legs and hands. In his unexpected excitement, he ripped the sack wide open. What fell out caused Gassy to turn as white as his underpants were before this moment.

The being inside was a horrific homunculus of gnome and hurgle. This wasn't the case of part gnome, part toad. No, this was much worse. In its brief gestation period, the baby had encountered the conundrum of which parent's limbs to adopt. It was also cursed with Gassy's indecisiveness. So, as a compromise, it chose to adopt both of their limbs. Gassy's new-born baby had two unique sets of legs and two unique sets of arms with a mix between the warty skin of the hurgle and the pale hairlessness of Gassy. Its face, however, was the most horrifying of all. It thought the best combination was to use Gassy's exact face, swapping out just one feature, the hurgle's enormous eyes. Eyes the size of a fist. Eyes that were now uncomfortably slotted into Gassy's relatively small head.

The horror wasn't over yet. After being born, hurgle babies reach maturity incredibly quickly. It's also why most are considered unintelligent, when they're usually just quite young.

"PwaaaPya," the abomination groaned, sounding like it was already in a deep, torturous pain.

"Nope," Gassy responded as he turned around and walked away.

"Where're ya goin'?" the hurgle mother called out. Gassy ignored them, but he couldn't ignore the fast-growing creature that hurried after him.

"Pahpuh!" it gurgled.

"Still nope," Gassy yelled back as his walk turned into a sprint. Around him, the busy marketplace made way for the chase with a level of disgust on their face Gassy had never seen before. He didn't know where he was running, but he went as fast as his little legs would take him.

Before long, Gassy had reached the only paved road in the town. In the time it took for him to get there, his new child had grown twice the size. It was now almost as tall as Gassy himself.

"Don' run pahpa!" it beckoned as its unnervingly deep voice found the right words.

"Don't chase!"

As he crossed the road his eyes darted up and down the street. He couldn't find anywhere to run. He couldn't see any help. Glancing back, all he could see was a mess. *Why did I leave my cosy little wizard's tower?* he thought to himself. Just then, something miraculous happened. A gift from the gods, or so Gassy would later think.

As this new hurgle rushed over the road, it failed to look both ways despite its disgustingly large eyes. As a result, it was immediately trampled and crushed by a horse and cart. Its internal organs were all squished to the back end resembling a spider's abdomen and its Gassy-like face crumpled in terror-filled pain. Gassy watched as this creature with his own face died. It didn't know why. Due to the incredibly young age of the hurgle, it was unable to learn one of life's vital lessons: road safety. As he stewed on his horrific experience, Gassy had only one thought on his mind, *I hope Borty's had more luck.*

Chapter Three

"What a sight to behold!" Borty bellowed to himself. He had to yell just to hear himself over the sheer noise of a room full of drunk Abitmorrians.

The pub Borty found himself in was a rather respectable inn the last time he visited, but they seemed to have gone through a few changes. Changes he was quite fond of. The day-drinking was about the same, but they had introduced some new entertainment: to his left was a small stage, likely used for dancing and singing; to the right, all sorts of gambling could be done; and in the centre, a fighting ring. The most popular of all was, of course, the most violent.

Borty's eyes lit up at the sight of so many vulnerable pockets, but any thieving plans were discouraged by the only person to have noticed him. Less of a person, more of a creature. It seemed the inn had improved their security by hiring an eldersnatch. Less grandiose than the name might suggest, eldersnatches were named as such after the first one discovered was found carrying three elderly people under one arm. Nothing but good intentions mind you, though that didn't stop the name spreading. After centuries of fine diplomacy and all-round good-boy behaviour, these keen-eyed goliaths have proven their stereotype to be far from true. Yet, the name remains.

"Better not!" Borty thought to himself aloud.

"Hey you! Aren' you s'posed to be fightin'?" a less than friendly voice queried.

"What?" Borty rebutted with his own powerful ponder.

"Geh back in the rin'. I've goh puzzle pieces on you."

Once he'd cottoned on, Borty changed his demeanour immediately. "I'm afraid you are most mistaken good sir"

"Miss taken? You's a gnome aren' you?"

"Incorrect my dear fellow. I am fae, dontyouknow."

"My apologies sir. I didn' mean noffin by it," the simple man responded.

"Not to worry. Off you go now. Must'nt've wasted our day on such myatters." Although Borty's impression wasn't exactly flawless, most common idiots couldn't much tell the difference. And so, off the man went. Not to think of Borty again.

"Ugh," Borty sighed. Impersonating a fae always made him feel dirty. He just hated pretending to be one of those poncy little bastards. They think they're all that, acting high and mighty, just because they have tiny wings and know a little about essence or magic or whatever they called it. He wouldn't pull out the fae card if he didn't have to, but for some reason people in small towns just don't question fae. Not as much as they would a gnome anyway. Still, he didn't have time to waste, so he sucked up his pride, stuck out his arse, and strutted around the room like he owned the place.

Gong, Gong, Gong. Hughey's calling caused half of the pub's occupants to harmonise in a collective "Awww," while the other half laughed at the misery of their employed companions slinking back to work.

"Pardon me fellow patrons," said Borty as he squeezed through the now dissipating crowd around the fighting ring. He effortlessly nabbed a pint from a man too drunk to notice his beer was missing. As he edged closer to the fight, he caught a glimpse of a terrorhawk. A nasty little flightless bird, the terrorhawk has claws designed for gutting. Get caught in its wings and it'll open up your belly like peeling a banana. He pitied the idiot dumb enough to fight one.

"C'mon Turdlet, you scrappy little bugger!" one eager fan shouted.

Of course it would be Turdlet. Why would it be anyone else? Turdlet was far from stupid, but he just didn't care. Which is likely why, when Borty finally got a good view, it seemed Turdlet was winning. A terrorhawk didn't quite know how to deal with an opponent that just didn't care if he was gutted or not.

"Don't die, you silly bastard!" Borty yelled.

The remaining crowd bellowed and screamed at the display of violence in the ring. Each time there was a blood splatter or a significant blow the crowd roared even louder. Just as Borty was getting into it, Turdlet spotted him.

"Borty Beetle-bowel!" he beamed as he launched the bird over his shoulder into one of the unsuspecting punters. "What're you doing here?"

Borty tried his best to ignore the many cuts and gashes across Turdlet's body. "Hey there...buddy. When you have a moment to talk, let me know."

"Oh sure! I can talk." Turdlet leaned on the edge of the ring. Behind him, a handful of day-drinkers did their best to fend off the terrorhawk.

"Are you sure you shouldn't sort that out?"

"Nahhh. That can wait. What brings you here?"

"The same thing that brings you here."

"Oh cool! You're going to wrestle a giant bird too?"

"No, I don't mean exactly the same. Adventure! That's what I mean. Excitement, intrigue, and plenty of reward!"

"You want help stealing something, say no more," said Turdlet as he hopped out the ring. He quickly threw on an old blood-stained shirt and paced over to a pew repurposed as a bench.

"I appreciate your eagerness, Turdlet, but I don't want to stir anything up. We're on a time-limit and I can't risk getting arrested."

"Yeah, bit late for that really. You can't really comprehend the level of trouble I've stirred up here already. Best we just leave while we can, eh." Turdlet launched his foot through the bottom of the hollow pew and pulled out a small backpack and a variety of weapons.

"I see. You've done something horrible, haven't you?" Borty's head filled with flashbacks too numerous to count. After deciding those thoughts best be saved for a spinoff, Borty's mind bounced back to the present where he pondered the extent of Turdlet's mess this time.

"Yeah, best not dwell on it," said Turdlet, "off we go."

On the way out the door, the innkeeper barked at the pair. "Oi! You fievin' li'le gnomes. You still owe fowsands on your tab. Get back 'ere!"

With a hop and a skip, Borty and Turdlet were past the eldersnatch and out of the pub, but not without a sizable tail. They ran as fast as they could, but knew it could be just a matter of time before they were caught.

"You drank thousands worth on a tab? How did you do that?! It's a piece per pint!" queried Borty as he realised he was still holding a beer, downing the remainder in seconds.

"That's not the question you should ask. What you should be asking me is, 'what idiot accepts a thousand beers on a tab?' Even a *councilman*, lower and upper, would have to pay that tab." Turdlet paused to throw Borty's empty glass at the innkeeper's head.

"Huh, you sneaky little gnomehead. How did you spin that one then?"

"I just pretended to be a different gnome every time I went in. It took them months to realise what I was doing," laughed Turdlet.

"It's always impressive what you are capable of getting away with until you stop getting away with it," said Borty.

"Gassy Bedchambers!" Turdlet exclaimed as they passed a terrible traffic accident. Gassy was shuffling along the road, barely a few steps from the corpse of his son, caught in a spiral of regret when he turned to see the pub escapees.

"Turdlet? Turdlet. That's who we came here for. You seriously trust *him*?" The tubby little gnome was clearly in no mood for a reunion with a borderline abusive acquaintance.

"Don't act like you aren't happy to see me." Turdlet spotted the hurgle crying at the corpse of its child. "You're as skilled with the ladies as ever, I see."

"Angry mob. Run now," a short-of-breath Borty commanded.

Stopping their chatter, the trio jumped into a sprint. They took every corner they could, losing a few pursuers but somehow the mob just kept growing. Hope was running thin alongside them as their options of escape fumbled, one after another. Escape cart? Nope, nobody would help them. Distraction? No way, they were *already* the distraction. As they exhausted another chance, Borty spotted something.

"A donkey! We're saved!" he yelled, sprinting towards it.

"That... donkey...isn't... going..." Each word Gassy said put him closer to blacking out. They'd probably ran at least half a mile by now.

"Yeah, we aren't getting anywhere on that," added Turdlet.

"Don't be stupid. We'll just fly away." Borty insisted, "Get on." He offered his hand after straddling the donkey.

"That's a different...donkey... it won't have wings...again."

"Again? You're both delusional. Donkey's don't have wings..." said Turdlet as the donkey stretched out its wings in front of him.

"Quick! Get on!" demanded Borty as the mob got closer. Without any more hesitation, they hopped on the back and the donkey took off, much to everyone's surprise (other than Borty's of course).

Once they were clear of arrows, Turdlet spoke up. "This ain't normal. Even coming from me, this really *is* unexpected. Donkeys can't do this."

"Not you too. I can't believe all the heists we've done together and I didn't realise how obsessed you two are with donkeys. Really it's just u–" Borty's little intervention was interrupted by a goring explosion from the town.

"Flipping heck!" exclaimed Gassy.

"The pub! The pub just blew up!" Borty yelled. "We were just in there!"

"Oh yeah. Weird," responded Turdlet.

"Turdlet. Why did that pub just blow up?"

"Dunno. Crazy." Turdlet had an obvious tell when he was lying. One-word sentences. It was something all of his friends, and most of his acquaintances, were aware of. On occasion, this rule conveniently extends to two words for the sake of storytelling.

"How did you do that? I was with you as we left, I didn't see you set anything up." Borty was more impressed than disappointed.

"He was probably planning to blow it up and you just happened to be there," added Gassy.

"Yeah, I was just planning on blowing it up and you just happened to be there."

"Right. Wonderful. From this point forward, no blowing anything up without discussing it with the group. Got it?" asked Borty.

"No explosions, got it," said Gassy.

"Fine," Turdlet added.

"Good. Now it's a long flight from here to our destination, best settle in."

* * * * *

By now, or indeed much earlier than now, some of you might be wondering to yourselves 'Why are there so many references to bottoms? This author seems obsessed. There really is an awful lot of it.'

I'm writing this now to assure you that you aren't going mad. You're right. There is a heck of a lot of tooshie talk. More specifically, all of the gnomes' names. This may seem entirely unnecessary, but there's a reason for it. In gnome culture, your derriere is sacred.

'What kind of cop-out is that?' you may say. A rather lazy one, but it's true. You see, gnomes have a very specific birth. Unlike most other beings, gnomes just pop out the ground one day. No babies. No puberty. They slowly gestate underground, taking all the nutrients from around them like a weed, and then emerge as fully-grown adults. Fully grown, for a gnome, is about three feet tall. Four if you're lucky.

What does this have to do with bums?

Other than the premature discovery of these little ground dwellers being reminiscent of uncovering a natural gas deposit, the first part of a gnome to emerge of its own accord is always the botty, without fail. Nobody quite knows why, but this is why naming a gnome after a pooper is the done thing.

Regardless, now's a pretty good time to grab yourself a cup of tea. Maybe have a mid-afternoon nap, or leave the bathroom and go back downstairs to the awkward dinner you've been avoiding. Don't worry, the story won't go on without you. Our little band of mischiefs will be travelling while you're gone and, by the time you're back, they'll only be a day away.

Chapter Four

"Boy, what an amazing couple of days," chirped Gassy, "a real adventure!"

"You're right about that, Gassy. Really an unforgettable journey," added Borty.

"I'm glad you fellas decided to pull me into this one. I would have hated to have missed such an eventful few days." Turdlet giggled to himself as he reminisced at all the fun things they'd done so far. So many memories in such a short time. "Shame about the donkey though."

"Well there's still more to come, gents," Borty paused as he prodded the dwindling campfire, "not long now until we reach Crimicon."

"When does it start? I hope we get there early. I really don't want to miss out on any collectibles."

"Don't you worry, Gassy," Borty began, "we should still arrive on opening day. They'll announce the category and target midday."

"I bloody hope it's not another sabotage request. It's been years since I did one that didn't require sneaking around like some hoighty toighty thieves' guilder."

"Now hold on there, Turdlet. Just because you weren't classically trained doesn't mean you can pick on those of us that were," said Gassy.

"I'll pick on whoever I feel like, you stinky squash-shaped ballsack." Although his vocabulary was limited, and his insult fairly unimaginative, his threatening sincerity made Turdlet's abuse just that bit more hurtful.

Feelings wounded, and self-confidence bruised, Gassy quietly slunk back into his tent. It was the only tent between the three and he refused to share. He'd spend the next few hours whimpering as he held himself. Thank goodness he brought a travel-sized erotica to comfort him.

"Why d'you have to be like that?" asked Borty.

"Like what?" Turdlet took a bite from his singed dinner.

"Just a real twat. You always poke fun at our Gassy, even though you know he's a sensitive soul."

"No, actually, I poke fun at him *because* he's a sensitive soul."

"That doesn't make it any better. I think that probably makes it worse," pondered Borty. He struggled to find the answer to that quandary with such a shaky moral compass. Borty and Turdlet both struggled with their sense of direction, morally speaking. They'd often lose themselves. Yet, they didn't seem too lost now.

"Have I ever told you about my friend Gravy?" asked Turdlet.

"Gravy? Gravy Scones, the sailor?"

"No, different Gravy. He's human."

"Then no I don't think so." Borty shuffled a little closer to the fire as he paid quick attention to Turdlet.

"Me and Gravy go way back. He was probably one of the first few people I met after I was born. He made a good living as a travelling musician and that's how I met him. The guy sang like he gargled the spent pennies of the gods every morning. Bloody beautiful it was. I bumped into him a good few times on the road, and every time people fell to their knees as he sang. Everyone wanted to be like him. But there was something everyone knew about him." Turdlet paused for dramatic effect.

"And that was?" Borty leant in closer.

"Gravy was simply the worst. Truly unbearable. He was loud, unhygienic, and vulgar. He made advances on *everyone* that was in his radius and most of those advances were instantly physical. He spat on people, he punched people, and he loved to flash people in public. He was the kind of guy that would make rubbish jokes and laugh at them louder than anyone else. All equally terrible things. And none of this really bothered me. What I hated, was that he thought we were friends. No matter how many times I said I didn't like him, he would pretend we were best buds. I'm not about to be just anyone's friend." Turdlet paused. He stared at Borty who was expecting more. "And do you know what the moral of this short story is?"

"No. What?"

"The moral is: as unbearable and unlikeable as Gravy was, I *still* prefer him to Gassy."

Throwing his hands up in the air, Borty was on the verge of punching Turdlet. "Would you kindly go screw yourself Turdlet. I was convinced you were actually going somewhere with that."

"If I went anywhere, it would preferably be away from Gassy."

"You don't really mean that," said Borty, "you're just worried about him getting hurt. He had some time off, but he's not useless."

"I'm not worried about *him* getting hurt. I'm actually hoping he'll get hurt. What I'm worried about is him getting *us* hurt."

"Turdlet, I know you better than you think. He's a smart kid and he's going to be okay. We'll all be fine."

Turdlet rolled onto his back and stared up into the sky. "Whatever happens, he's your responsibility now."

In the quiet of the forest around them, Borty and Turdlet explored the luminescent sky. They lay in a small clearing surrounded by tall pine trees that softened the sound of a nearby trickling stream that horseshoed around the camp. Above them, the night sky was furrowed by the encroaching pine needles. It was calming. Nice, even. Those were the thoughts that ran through Borty's head. Thoughts that quickly confused him.

What was nice? He thought to himself. It wasn't like this was his first time in a forest. In fact, he'd spent much of the past few months in a forest, only returning from them after hearing about the Crimicon and its Crimicompetition. So, his thoughts circled back. *What's nice? Why do I feel so content?*

It wasn't long before his wondering mind translated into wondering eyes, skipping across the stars. Borty marvelled at all the colours coming from clouds both cosmic and atmospheric. Their swirls soothed him. The simmering crackles of the fire, the whispering rustles of the occasional tumbling leaf, the soft wheezing of Turdlet's shallow slumber. They all soothed him. Comforts that carried him until, he too, was asleep.

* * * * *

The morning hit quickly. Like a cockerel's crow would attack the ears, a branch attacked Borty's face, multiple times. He opened his eyes. They slowly adapted to the morning light to reveal Turdlet standing over him with a branch, hitting him softly. Just as Borty was about to take a breath to scold him for his odd behaviour, Turdlet pressed a finger against his lips. To be clear, Turdlet's finger was pressed against Borty's lips. As uncomfortable as this may seem, Borty understood.

Gassy squatted behind the pair in a silent panic, shaking. His back was pressed up against a tree. Borty could hear screaming. Looking past Gassy, Borty saw what had gotten the previously jovial gnomes so worked-up.

"A war-party," whispered Borty. His spontaneous thought-to-mouth resulted in the others flailing and flourishing their arms in distress. Turdlet grabbed him by the collar, dragged him to the tree Gassy found shelter under, and pointed to a perfect line-of-sight through the thicket. As if framed by nature itself, Borty spotted an enforcer, an endlessly loyal bodyguard dedicated to an upper councilmember. If Borty held any doubt which councilmember the enforcer belonged to, the golden sun sigil on his chest plate was evidence enough. He was a light stroller. He belonged to the upper councilmember, Day Lord.

The enforcer's legendary military-might was put on show as he separated a nearby heavily-armed militiaman from his own legs. This goliath was temporarily apologetic until he did the exact same thing to an unarmed villager.

Immediately, without a question in his mind, Borty started to slink away from the slaughter before he was directed to yet another important detail. Printed on the side of a factory house were the words 'Sponsored by MagInc'.

MagInc? he thought to himself, *why are they attacking MagInc?* Day Lord—and all the other members of the upper council for that matter—made unsurmountable mountains of profit from their relationship with MagInc. So, it begged the question, *what did Day Lord have to gain from raiding MagInc?*

Confused, the gnomes slowly edged away from the combat. There was nothing they could do. This became more apparent when they bumped into someone else in the woods who was also watching the massacre, only they seemed to be a touch more upset about it.

Standing with a small knife in hand, and a couple rabbits in the other, a rather young boy watched in tears. For a moment, the gnomes froze. They didn't know how to react. Gassy began a silent argument with the others, insisting they take the boy with them. It was a kind choice. One that would likely save his life. Approaching him carefully, Borty tried to avert the child's gaze by distracting him with chaotic hand movements. His display looked more like the mating dance of a wounded bird of paradise, but it did what was intended. With the boy's attention, there was little need for signed persuasion before the gnomes were able to steer him away from Day Lord's light strollers.

At the edge of the nearest main road, the gnomes and their new-found friend sat waiting for a traveller kind enough to give them a lift. After almost an hour of waiting, Borty was pacing back and forth in front of the others.

"This is ridiculous. Not even a single donkey in all this time."

"What's ridiculous is you're expecting a donkey to come down that road. Literally nobody but us seems to travel by donkey," said Gassy

"That's it," declared Borty, "we can't just sit around. Day Lord's light strollers were right there."

"They won't hurt us," said Gassy who was doing his best to simultaneously calm Borty and himself down, "Day Lord doesn't just attack people randomly. He's a member of the upper council, for flip's sake. Those people back there must have done something to deserve it."

"You mean like you did?" asked Turdlet.

"Turdlet, don't be so insensitive," said Borty.

Gassy's posture slumped into a gelatinous mess. He stared through the ground, as if he was trying to see what lay six feet below.

"Day Lord doesn't forgive. You wrong him, you best be ready to pay the price. I was prepared enough to escape his punishment, but those MagInc workers clearly weren't."

"And how about your crew? Were they prepared to escape?"

"Turdlet, don't," said Borty.

"I warned my crew over and over," said Gassy, "they refused to listen about the dangers of stealing from Day Lord and they all suffered for it. I imagine it's the same for these people."

The young boy was scratching his knife in the ground, drawing circles and digging holes. Whenever the topic of his village came up, his playing became notably more forceful.

Borty looked up and down the road again. He seemed to be on the precipice of a decision. He commanded everyone's attention. Even the wind stopped for him. "That's it! We're walking."

A chorus of disappointed noises came from the group of gnomes. "Please don't make me walk," begged Gassy.

"No. It's decided. We're walking."

"What about the boy?"

"The boy can come too. I'm not heartless, we'll just drop him off at the town's orphanage when we get there." Borty strode over to his things and started to gather them.

Struggling to think of a reason to avoid walking for miles, Gassy said, "But we don't even know his name. We can't just take a child without even knowing its name."

"His name's Timmy," Turdlet declared.

After a brief moment of confusion, Borty spoke up, "How do you know his name? He hasn't spoken a word since we picked him up."

"Of course his name's Timmy. Pretty much every orphan is called Timmy." Nobody ever learned why Turdlet came to this conclusion. It wasn't common knowledge like he insisted it was. We can only assume he mixed up two rather famous Dickensian characters but we'll never truly know. This particular topic would actually go on to be a point of debate in taverns across the country, seemingly coincidentally. It would become so prevalent in popular culture that people started to use Timmy as a synonym to mean 'a persistent incorrect thought' where it could be heard in such sentences as: 'He's got a timmy that she's taken a liking to him,' or 'That man's wealth of timmies is going to be the death of him.' As a somewhat cruel joke that became commonplace, people also started to name their unwanted – or unexpected – children Timmy regardless of gender. But for our gnome-based conundrum, a quick back and forth between the boys led them to an agreed conclusion.

"Fine! We'll call him Timmy," announced Borty. "Nice to meet you, Timmy."

"Cheer up, Timmy," said Gassy. It was less of a comforting tone and more like a request after not knowing what to say. "We'll look after you."

"I don't trust him," Turdlet whispered to Borty.

Matching his tone, Borty responded, "It's a child. What could you possibly be worried he'll do?"

"Murder someone. He's definitely going to murder someone."

"I sometimes really worry about you. The things you must have seen to assume that."

"Well, well, well. If it isn't the...some...a group of idiots," taunted an all too familiar voice, antagonistically.

As Gassy helped Timmy off the ground, Borty turned to see a group of smirking, faceless goons standing in a clearly choreographed pose. One gnome-it-all stood in the centre, posing even smirkier than the others. His rich plum-coloured cloak fluttered in the wind. He had a very unusual face. His eyes, ears, teeth, and nose all seemed to have the same mission in mind; get as far away from his face as possible.

"Breezy. Of course we had to bump into you." Borty was midway towards a growl.

"Hardly a bump. We saw you on the side of the road, like a peasant. I assume you are heading to Crimicon too? Good luck getting there, whereas I'll be travelling in style." Breezy gestured towards a wonderfully ornate and spacious carriage with the words 'Sponsored by MagInc' printed on the side. The carriage was the latest model known as the MagInc Skyskimmer™, a spiritual successor to their Moonjumper™ line. Breezy's particular model came with all the trimmings: the crystal-heated carriage seats, the built-in safety pillows in case of a crash, even the stain-resistant lining for when the carriage reaches the vomit-inducing speed of 30mph.

41

"Working for MagInc now? And here I thought you couldn't stoop any lower."

"Stoop? How ignorant. MagInc are taking the forgotten tradition of thievery to the masses. In just a few short years, everybody will know what it is like to be stolen from on a day-to-day basis. They are visionaries." Breezy's smugness grew with every sentence that oozed out of his mouth.

"Thieving and murdering is a time-honoured tradition that takes years to master. You can't just start nabbing things on day one. You've got to earn it," argued Turdlet. Not many things got him riled, but jeopardising the honour amongst thieves was apparently one of them.

"Your archaic ideas will never last, Turdless."

Without a breath, Turdlet pulled a miniature crossbow from behind him and aimed it right at Breezy's head. Just as he pulled the trigger, Borty pushed his arm towards the sky causing the bolt to fly far from its target.

"Nice shot," chuckled Breezy. After a brief delay, and some encouragement, his entourage mimicked his chuckle.

Borty dragged Turdlet to one side to whisper-shout at him, "We can't afford beef with MagInc right now. You'll just have to suck it up."

"Just let me kill him. He's a poncy prick that deserves a good spear up his arse."

"You could not hurt me even if you wanted to," smarmed Breezy. "My essence-catalyst is far too powerful for you to comprehend."

"It's a magic wand," sniped Turdlet.

"No, it is not!" yelled Breezy. "It is an essence-catalyst, converting the very power that surrounds us into pure, unadulterated energy."

"The power around us? You mean, magic? So, it's a magic wand then." Few people could get under Turdlet's skin like Breezy, but the same could be said both ways.

"No! Stop saying that," Breezy's voice cracked as he protested against such a mediocre title for his weapon. "I would not be caught dead using a wand. Look at the pure chicness of this remarkable handcrafted tool." Breezy pulled his essence-catalyst from his side and marvelled at its design.

"You're a handcrafted tool." Turdlet taunted under his breath as he noticed Borty staring daggers at him.

"That is it!" barked Breezy. "We have already wasted enough time on you. We are leaving. I hope a cart crushes you all. Except for you, Gassy."

Gassy jumped when his name was mentioned. He looked around, then pointed to himself with wide eyes.

"Perhaps when you are done wasting your time with these oafs," continued Breezy, "you should consider signing up with MagInc. They would never waste a classically trained artist such as yourself." Breezy strode back to his carriage with the most punchable expression plastered across his face.

"What an unbearable c—"

"Guys, the carriage!" exclaimed Borty, interrupting Turdlet's potty mouth.

"Yeah we know. It's a very nice carriage. I guess that's the reward you get for brown-nosing the corporate elite," said Turdlet.

"No, look at all that space on the back. It could fit all of us." Borty's observation was very astute. It indeed could fit everyone on the back, including Timmy, for it was the MagInc Skyskimmer™ with all the extra add-ons. Additions such as: the captured fairy soul for easy cruise control, the springbug suspension for smooth rides, and the expanded trunk for more of your junk.

Without another word, everyone hurried after the carriage before it gained some speed. The whole gang effortlessly slipped into the back to find the most comfortable confined space they'd ever been in. And boy were they familiar with confined spaces. It was a long ride from here, and they all knew not to make a whisper, so they took their chance to get some shut-eye.

Chapter Five

"*Fire!*" a voice commanded from outside the storage box.
Not a breath later and the calm was split open by the
crackling of essence-based weapons. Their mixture of
prepared spells shattered with different rumbles of impact.

"Ooo ruddy dora!" Gassy yelped as he thumped his
chunky head on the cargo space's ceiling. "What in the gods
was that?!"

"Shhh!" Turdlet's hushing was even louder than Gassy's
frightened exclamation.

"Shut it, both of you," whispered Borty, "there's a fight
going on outside."

He lifted up the lid of their hiding spot and a slither of
fading sunlight squeezed in. They weren't moving anymore
and they immediately spotted the reason. A few dozen guards
were attacking a snugglebumble. The biggest one any of them
had ever seen.

Like most creatures in the human realms, the snugglebumble was aptly named. However, it isn't quite as fluffy and cute as the name suggests. It can certainly be considered adorable in some aspects, but its nature tends to take away from any aesthetic quality the snugglebumble has. The primary drive of any simple-minded snugglebumble is collecting scents. Any scent will do. They use these unique scents to both attract a mate and mark territory. Fairly straightforward so far, and perfectly innocent when they're no larger than a grapefruit. The trouble comes when they reach a certain size. You see, in order to collect scents, the snugglebumble has developed a tactic of latching onto the thing it's particularly fond of that year and violently vibrating, and nobody quite knows the limit of their size.

With that knowledge in mind, you can understand why the gnomes sat in stunned horror watching this snugglebumble – the size of a small house – leap from guard to guard, pulverising them into a liquefied gooey mess.

"Cover the child's eyes," Gassy suggested, as he covered his own eyes. To his right, Timmy sat in a mix between shock and awe. He'd never seen something so graphic. Not even the recent massacre of his village was so violent.

"Why would Breezy stop here of all places?" asked Borty, with no reasonable response from anyone. "I'm going to get out and check."

"No, Borty. Don't risk it," whimpered Gassy from behind his hands. "We should just stay in the cart."

"I'm coming too," said Turdlet as he joined Borty in ignoring Gassy and hopping out of the carriage.

The moment they hit the ground they could see why they'd stopped, the horse pulling the carriage was almost exclusively goop. Looking ahead, Borty could see a path of destruction that had blasted along half a mile, from the forest into the main road. The place was packed with carriages, many of which also had goopy horses. Much to his disappointment, he could see Breezy had been escorted out of his carriage to safety nearby.

"Alright, everyone out. This is going to take a while and we aren't safe here."

"I feel safer here," insisted Gassy.

"You don't have a choice in the matter, Gassy. C'mon, Timmy, you too," commanded Borty.

"Where're we headed, Borty?" Turdlet queried as he noticed no direction was particularly appealing. If there were snugglebumbles in the area, even a horse-sized one was enough to pop everyone in the party. The forest was out of the question.

"Let's head up the road on foot. It's only a couple mile—"

"CITIZEN," yelled a muscle-bound foot soldier. He was standing beside everyone. "IT IS MY DUTY TO ENSURE YOUR SAFETY. DO NOT RESIST OR I WILL HAVE TO USE FORCE."

"Lords he's loud. He's even speaking in caps." Turdlet picked at his ears.

"We're fine, mate. We'll take care of ourselves," said Borty, fully understanding what a soldier's version of 'safety' was for a citizen.

"I dunno. I think we should get Gassy to safety. He couldn't even handle this soldier." Turdlet's 'concern' didn't fit his smiling face. Borty almost immediately knew where Turdlet's mind was going.

"Seriously though, Turdlet, Gassy is a bit soft. We really shouldn't use hi—"

"Hey!" interjected Gassy. "I'm not soft. I can do anything Turdlet can do."

"You don't even know *what* I'm doing most days," taunted Turdlet.

"Shut up!" yelled Gassy.

"Gassy, don't let him get to you. It's alright to know your weaknesses."

"CITIZENS. I WILL NEED TO ESCORT YOU TO SAFETY NOW." His monotonous yelling was almost soothing compared to what was behind him. The snugglebumble now fumbled through a soldiers' huddle, causing them to crumple into a muscle-puddle. So fierce was the trouble that even the sentences describing it buckled into a humble rubble.

"Yeah, solid idea, soldier guy." Turdlet glanced at Gassy's growing fidgeting with each word. "Maybe you should take Gassy though. He's slow, and doughy. The snugglebumble'll have no problem rolling his malleable body into a nice, soft flatbread."

"Stop it Turdlet! I'm not slow *or* doughy."

"You know what? You're right, Gassy," began Turdlet, piquing Gassy's interest, "I'd more accurately describe you as brittle. Even though you look like a scoop of half-melted ice-cream, you're actually quite coarse and incredibly inflexible."

Borty caught himself nodding along with Turdlet.

"I'm not weak! I'm not doughy or misshapen or slow or pathetic or disappointing..." began Gassy.

"Added a couple extras there, bud." Borty stifled a laugh. He was trying not to take sides but sometimes Gassy made it so hard.

"It's not fair. You always pick on me! Both of you. The only reason our heists ever work is because of my quality planning, but you always call me things like ball sack or some other piece of genitalia."

"You have to know that's not entirely true. We often don't follow your plan." Borty's comment seemed to hurt Gassy more than any of the judgements Turdlet made. Gassy stared through his companions. Turdlet had won.

"CITIZEN. I AM GOING TO HAVE TO ASK YOU TO CALM YOURSELF. WE ARE IN A COMBA—"

"FRICK OFF, will you!" Gassy heartily demanded in a mimicking tone. In the same sentence, Gassy quickly unsheathed a hidden knife from his cloak. No thicker than a thick knife and no thinner than a thin knife, the knife spent less than a second outside its sheath before it was plunged comfortably inside the thigh of the mouthy soldier. Although girth was no problem for this knife, the length was really underwhelming. The soldier could barely feel Gassy wiggling it around inside him, expressing little but a hybrid of minor discomfort and plenty of pity.

In the silence after, Gassy realised his mistake. The screams of people dying liquidy deaths could be very clearly heard but paired with this rather distinct sound was a gnomey high-five shared between Turdlet and himself, also known as a high-clap. Turdlet knew what came next.

"CITIZEN. YOU ARE UNDER ARREST," screeched the soldier, putting an unusual amount of stress on the 'st' at the end of 'arrest'. He then pulled a bludgeon from his side.

"No... wait..." pleaded Gassy, realising what was happening.

"STOP RESISTING," the soldier yelled as he began to wallop Gassy with generous force. *Crack* became a familiar sound in a short time. Whether it was Gassy's bones or the bludgeon tiring, many cracks could be heard. Borty and Turdlet watched, unfazed as their friend was beaten to a pulp. Once the soldier had decided he was good and 'restrained', he placed Gassy under arrest.

"Arrest us too! We're his accomplices," stated Turdlet as he put his arms forward. Borty sighed as he looked at the bloody mess that was Gassy.

"We'd like to peacefully turn ourselves in. The boy is also—" began Borty, "wait. Where'd Timmy go?"

As the soldier cuffed the much healthier gnomes, Turdlet said, "He's probably part of the blood puddle. Best not let it get to you Tthese things happen."

"Yeah. I suppose there's no point crying over spilt blood."

Once the gnomes were all cuffed, the soldier escorted them away from the danger and into a jailer's cart, dragging an unconscious Gassy through the bloodied mud all the way. The moment the door was closed behind them, the cart sped off towards the town leaving the 'rescued' to moan at the side of the road.

* * * * *

Waking up in a jail cell wasn't something the gnomes were unfamiliar with. Even the less experienced of the group, Gassy, still managed to find time to get himself arrested in his younger years. They'd all learned to find their comforts where they could. The uniformity of the cells made it easier. When your country's government and military receive most of their architectural designs, building materials, and security all from the same company while shunning any sense of meaningful regulation, breaking out of one jail is just like breaking out of any other. Borty would go as far as to say they were experts.

This particular jail was your standard-issue minimum security, barely a few bars in a window held them back from the streets themselves. Then there was of course the door to their cage. It had some unique decorative carvings to it, but the lock was incredibly basic. They didn't even bother with enchantments.

After a cosy forced-nap, Gassy awoke to find his body in better condition than expected. He wasn't completely healed up, by any means, but what he anticipated to be serious injuries turned out to be nothing more than a few meaningful bruises and a sore belly.

"What happened?" he said.

"We got lucky," said Borty.

Borty was lying on what seemed to be a freshly-purchased, double-quilted, mushroomfoam mattress. Pure luxury. At the end of the bed, Turdlet was hunched over an impressive helping of plantegg. A plantegg – unlike the eggplant you may be more familiar with – is a large plant-shaped egg. Its appearance might resemble your everyday stick of celery but its rich, creamy centre is evidence of the plantegg belonging to the sentient humanoids, oakmites. You may think it's a bit barbaric to eat the eggs of sentient beings, but not all eggs are necessarily fertilized. What are they going to do? Just throw away a perfectly good plantegg? Why waste such a delicacy?

Mind cogs whirring, Gassy spoke up, "Hold on a moment. What's going on here? I thought this was a jail."

"It is," said Turdlet, creamy plantegg yolk dribbling down his chin.

"Then would you care to explain?" Gassy's patience was beginning to wear thin. Then their jail door opened.

"Hello gents," said the young guard. He was carrying all their equipment and tools that were confiscated by his comrades.

"Thanks Joel," said Borty.

"Oh no, you don't have to thank me. I'm sorry about the mix-up, I really didn't know you were allowed to keep all your things."

"Don't mention it," said Borty, "oh, and can you give us our privacy Joel? In fact, can you just step out for an hour or so? Maybe take your break and have a good time."

"Say no more," said Joel as he stepped out with a big smile. Before closing the door, he turned to Borty. "Promise you won't go anywhere?"

"Joel. Wouldn't dream of it," Borty smiled back. Joel, gaining as much air as joy can give a fully armoured man, skipped away after locking the door behind him.

"I'm honestly concerned for that guy," said Turdlet.

"What?" asked Gassy, he gestured to where Joel was with a frown on his face. He'd never quite seen someone fit the 'fresh out the academy' vibe so perfectly, and yet have no knowledge to show for it. Joel was clearly trying so hard, bless him.

"Hilarious, ain't it?" giggled Turdlet. "He just does whatever Borty asks." Putting his mostly finished plantegg to one side, Turdlet hopped up onto his feet and started fiddling with the heavy door lock. Ignoring him, Gassy started to inspect his own body. He lifted up his top and squeezed at all his soft spots.

"I'm so confused. Even if we ignore the dummy guard, why am I all fixed up?"

"Ask Turdlet." Borty paused for a moment. He and Gassy looked over to Turdlet who ignored the both of them to focus on his task at hand. Borty continued, "Turdlet was slightly concerned about you for a moment there. He asked me to fix you up, so I got our attentive servant to grab a little something to sort you out properly."

Gassy quickly grabbed the empty potion bottle at the end of his bed. He admired its majestic design, struggling to believe that Turdlet would think of anyone but himself. Then Gassy inspected the price on its label.

"Thirty thousand!" he exclaimed. He'd never seen regenerative remedies reach prices past ten thousand. This was some masterwork medicine, some high tier cocktail, some premium-grade shit. "Explain please."

"We didn't pay for it, if that's what you're worried about." Turdlet chimed in, tools still shimmying in the door lock.

"Yeah, Joel popped to the jail apothecary. Apparently, the apothecary here is insanely well stocked," said Borty.

Gassy squeezed his forehead like he was trying to squish his thoughts. "I almost died. Turdlet almost got me killed."

"You can't put all the blame on Turdlet. I didn't exactly help. But you have to admit his 'plan' worked. We got a quick ride to town and didn't get crushed in the process." Borty was punctuated by the click of the jail door unlocking. "Now you can sulk about his methods, or we can get on and do this job."

There was a pause. Gassy gave it a good think. Among those thoughts were ways he could get Turdlet beaten to a pulp to see how he liked it but, in the end, he took the more civilized approach.

"Fine. But you both owe me."

Chapter Six

Out on the street the gnome gang could finally appreciate where they were.

"Under-arraz ahhh," sighed Borty. Gassy and Turdlet also sighed. They sounded satisfied. It wasn't that they were, more that they knew the rules. They had to sound satisfied. You see, a long time ago a very controlling – very specific – and very petty queen once visited the large town of Under-arraz. Much to her surprise, her stay was positively stupendous. Completely without fault. No matter how hard she tried, and boy did she try, the queen found nothing out of place. So, in a decision that came to be largely regarded as regrettable, the queen insisted that whenever Under-arraz's name was mentioned, the mentioner and mentionees all had to give a sigh of relief. Failure to sigh would result in a fine of two hundred bluckles.

Some would say two hundred bluckles isn't that bad of a punishment, especially since the currency has been dead for almost a hundred years (the most recent currency being pieces to a giant, magical, golden puzzle) so the law was therefore impossible to enforce.

No, not a bad punishment at all.

However, the people of Under-arraz adapted the law just a little. The punishment evolved over the years from a reasonable fine to a significantly unreasonable mob murder. If anyone was caught saying Under-arraz without sighing, chances are they'd be bludgeoned to death by a rather cross crowd. This was a phenomenon that happened most commonly to tourists without much care for the traditions and the expectations of the town they stayed in, so not a big loss really.

"I really wish the Crimicon was in any other town than this one," said Gassy.

"Really? I love this town," said Borty.

"Not me. I have terrible memories of this place."

"Oh. Yeah, of course." Borty didn't really know what to say. They just stood in an awkward silence for moment.

"We should probably get a move on. We don't want to be standing outside our own jail cells when Joel comes back." Gassy tried to take his own words seriously, but one of the roads forking past the jailhouse was packed full of street meats and crop stands. His mouth was watering. He'd been dreaming about a place like this for a few days. That's not a comment on Gassy's unhealthy relationship with food, which he definitely has, it's more that the gnomes were yet to stop for something good to eat on their journey.

"No harm in just stopping off for a quick snack," said Turdlet as he edged towards the nearby street. With half-arsed resistance, Borty and Gassy followed behind.

"No harm at all. He practically just left," reasoned Gassy. They looked to Borty for permission.

"Let's be quick about it then, boys. The convention will be opening soon." Borty's sentence tapered off as he explored the scents of the greasy slabs of fatty mess that slid from grills all around him.

"Yeah. We'll just get something quick."

"Something quick sounds good."

Three hours passed. The gnomes didn't stop walking up and down Meat Street – named as such before they added in the veggie section. The busy crowds and diverse population meant they didn't have much trouble with anti-gnome behaviour. They were able to explore every possible meander of the road, marvelling at its unending selection of cuisines. Rainbows of different coloured vegetables, some twice their size, all looked like they would pair wonderfully with the immense selection of meats. Animals the gnomes had never even heard of. A tabblepap tongue, a wigsnop wing, a ghuhupht dewlap (pronounced like a displeased in-law clearing their throat). They even had snugglebumble which is essentially like eating spongey acid. Somewhere on the road, there was a stall or restaurant that used these ingredients. Not a single citizen in Under-arraz (sigh) bothered to cook at home. Why would they? They could have anything they wanted. So, what did the gnomes choose?

Nothing. The gnomes chose nothing. Three hours of walking through the immense selection, bags bursting with puzzle pieces they pocket-picked from patrons, and none of them even considered swiping so much as a morsel. Instead of making the decision of where to eat, they shuffled from stall to stall saying things like 'ooo no. Seafood doesn't agree with me,' and 'I'm not really in the mood for poached horse.'

As they returned for their second approach at the strip – likely planning to go to the first place they liked the look of all those hours ago – the gnomes were stopped by a surprised shriek.

"Hey! You're not supposed to be here!"

It was Joel. He was carrying a scarecrow, or at least that's what it looked like. It was in a little better condition that most scarecrows and had much nicer hair than most people. Even its eyelashes were pretty.

"Hi there, buddy. You were gone so long. We came looking for you." Borty wasn't in the mood to think of a good lie. He was barely in the mood to eat at this rate.

"Oh no you don't. You gnomes definitely shouldn't be here."

"That's racist," said Turdlet, forced disgust printed across his face.

"Yeah...racist." Gassy's contribution received mixed responses but he said it loud enough to get the attention of some passers-by.

"You all *promised* that you would stay in jail. How am I supposed to trust you now?"

"You mean, how are you supposed to trust the people that stabbed your boss in the leg?"

"Yes. You're not making it easy." Unfortunately for Joel, *he* was making it *very* easy. The gnomes almost felt bad. Gassy was particularly almost-guilt ridden. 'Almost-guilt' is a feeling Turdlet came up with when he decided he didn't like to be thought of as heartless but was also too lazy to pretend to feel guilty.

"So? What are you going to do about it, huh?" rhetorised Turdlet.

"Well... I'm going to arrest you. Yeah, that's right. I'm going to arrest you." By this point, they'd gathered the attention of a small crowd.

"No you're not," insisted Borty.

"Wah... yes I am!" Although his argument seemed sound, the guard was stunned by Borty's rebuttal.

"Nope."

"What do you mean? Yes, I am. Consider yourselves arrested."

"You're going the right way fo—" began Turdlet.

"I've got this one," interrupted Borty. He stepped towards the guard and said, "Consider ourselves what?"

"Consider yourselves arrested!" Joel shuffled his right hand around his body, struggling to find his sword with a 'scarecrow' in the other hand.

"A what?"

"Arrested!" he yelled.

"You're avesting me?" Borty's confusion was *only* convincing Joel.

"No! Arresting!" screamed Joel.

"Still not getting it. Can you say it faster?"

"You're under arres—"

Before he could even finish, the crowd around him sighed a pleasant hum. The silence after their agreeable outburst was deafening. They stared at him. Joel stared back. Faces turned from pleased to horrified. Over a dozen people stood, ignoring the gnomes completely, and glared at the guard. A few seconds passed. The civilians slowly revealed all sorts of weapons. Knives, axes, scythes, one guy even had a flail. Hesitantly, Joel finally found the hilt of his sword and slowly unsheathed it.

"Now, I don't know why you'd all choose to collude with these criminals, but I insist you all lay down your arms. If you don't, I shall be forced to put you all under arrest." In a flash, they swarmed him. Unsurprisingly, he was overwhelmed in a second. Doubly unsurprisingly, it was the fella with the flail that ended the boy's life. He put a hole where Joel's head should be.

"Wow. Still, that's a real shame," Gassy started as the crowd took turns brutalising Joel's body, "he seemed like a nice lad."

"At least I got these." Turdlet brandished a new set of chunky handcuffs with the town's insignia carved on.

"When did you nab those?!"

"I'll be honest, I don't even know. Sometimes my hands just take things without me thinking about it. But I'm sure they'll come in handy later on."

"I don't want to sound negative, but it might be a good idea if we don't hang around," said Gassy.

In agreement, the gnomes scurried off away from the crowds, swiping a variable assortment of snackables on the way.

* * * * *

Under-arraz (sigh) has always been a prosperous town. The word town would seem like an understatement to anyone that visited. It was clearly one of the greatest cities in the country. Yet, even after being much larger than many cities, Under-arraz (sigh) was never granted that status. Reasons varied. Some said you needed to have a university to make a town into a city, whereas Under-arraz (sigh) only 'technically' has colleges of higher education. Some people used the excuse that every city should have a royal palace, but Under-arraz (sigh) has a holy manor house instead. More extreme views blamed it on a lack of magic users, immigrants, or the repeating infestations of monkeyrats – a creature with as many arms as there are spellings for its name.

Whatever the real reason, it was a contention point for most under-arrazites with murderous civic pride. Most under-arrazites in general, actually. It was such a collective insecurity that citizens were banding together in droves to improve the attractiveness of the town. They tried everything. Painting every house a different pattern or colour: they didn't like that, so they tried painting streets with themes that blended them together. Citizens built monuments, carved statues, nurtured beautifully shaped shrubberies. They even hired magicians to cast a town-wide enchantment that made its streets self-cleaning and layered a beatifying filter across life in the town.

Even though their attempts to make the town stand out brought smiling faces to a few people, a loud majority were still unsatisfied. Under-arraz (sigh) deserved something special. And so, half a century ago, they figured it out. Ribbons. The town discovered ribbons. With all the remarkable options available to them in the twelve schools of magic, the under-arrazites decided the best step forward was ribbons. The ribbon became the symbol of the town. They implemented them in every possible way you can think of. Need a bed? Ribbons. Looking for somewhere to dry your laundry? Ribbons. Want to go to the local dance with someone but nobody wants to go with you? Ribbons. Cold? Ribbons. Hot? Ribbons. Ribbons? Ribbons.

So it went, for decades. Ribbons became so widely used within the town that the word itself was used to describe something perfect for the situation. An example would be, 'That grill was just the ribbon for my undercooked horse,' a sentence otherwise lost to most outsiders.

Yet, the most widely implemented use of ribbons travelled throughout the town. A navigator. Above every street hung hundreds of slightly different coloured – or patterned – ribbons. Each one led to somewhere. You could follow the wine-purple ribbon with gold trimmings right to the most expensive manor in town. Follow the navy-blue ribbon with white stripes and you'd arrive at the town's port. Or you could follow the plain crimson ribbon to Meat Street which happened to be the only place in town this waving stream of streamers chose to avoid after a grill-fire ignited the ribbons and put the whole street in flames, just ten years ago. Don't worry, nobody blamed the ribbons, it was clearly the chef's fault and he was swiftly put to death. Still, after the rebuild they redirected the ribbons so no fool would endanger them again.

This somewhat lengthy detour is all vital information in explaining why, when Borty materialised a flyer from his back pocket, he announced...

"Follow the black and green ribbon, with little horseshoes."

Chapter Seven

"It's a barn."

"No. That can't be right," pondered Borty. "It's a huge event. They can't keep it all in a barn."

The gnomes stood at the end of the black and green ribbon. Gassy was right. It was indeed attached to a barn.

"They were closed for a few years. Maybe they lost some funding," suggested Gassy.

"But MagInc has sponsored Breezy in this year's Crimicompetition. They wouldn't dare just throw away puzzle pieces like that."

"Look!" exclaimed Gassy, pointing to the out-of-this-world MagInc Skyskimmer™ tucked around the side of the barn, along with a few other inferior carriages.

"If Breezy's here, then we've gotta be in the right place." With no more hesitation Turdlet hurried towards the barn. Optimistically cautious, the others followed close-by.

Turdlet slid open the enormous door to reveal a near-empty barn with nothing but a cow, the pungent smell of that cow, some hay, and a sign that read:

'Welcome to CrimiCon: Under Four Feet'.

"That must be a typo, surely," Gassy said to Borty. "You told us the theme was four feet under."

"What does it matter? The place is empty. They must have moved location or something." Borty slumped, defeated, on the hay-covered floor.

"We came all this way. There must be a clue we can follow," said Gassy. Meanwhile, Turdlet took the chance to have some fun. As the others chatted away, he went for an explore and soon discovered a ladder. Without a second thought, he climbed up the ladder to the overhanging rafters of the barn to find little worth mentioning. Regrettably, once at the top Turdlet realised there was no down ladder. It was impossible to use the up ladder to go down. He was stuck. *Not a problem*, thought Turdlet, *I know just what to do.*

"Hey guys. Watch this!" He yelled from the half-attic. Without a chance to object, Borty and Gassy were forced to witness their friend launch himself off his platform, tuck into a ball, all the while yelling, "Cannonball!"

While Turdlet sinks through the air, there's something quite important to note. As you may have gathered by now, every gnome is a little special. No two gnomes are the same. Much like people. But we haven't quite gotten to what makes Turdlet so special. On first appearances you'd say, 'He's clearly the wildcard. The unpredictable element. The chaos that keeps things fun.' And yes, you would be correct in that assessment, but that's less of a characteristic and more of a convenient plot device to keep things moving. No, what makes Turdlet stand out from the crowd is something he's far from embarrassed to admit.

Turdlet has a botty made of metal.

In a very literal sense, Turdlet's cheeks of wonder are a marvellously chic pearlescent plating. He's figured that much of life's solutions can be solved by approaching them bum first which is especially true when you have buns of steel. The reason for such a resilient rectum can be summed up to Turdlet's rather unremarkable birth. Turdlet popped out of the ground one day, without much warning, much like every gnome before him. Turdlet, however, happened to be gestating in a field known for its bloody battles which resulted in Turdlet having an awful lot of iron in his system. Not knowing what to do with all this iron, his body sent it the only place it could, to his bum-bum. With this in mind, back to it.

"Catch him Borty!" bellowed Gassy, his hands half-hiding his face.

Borty sprinted as fast as he could, open-armed, trying to catch his friend. He was too late. Turdlet dropped through the air and split the floorboards wide open, sinking straight through them into darkness below.

"Ow! Ye fecker," an unlucky voice yelped from below.

"Turdlet?" called Gassy.

Silence.

"Turdlet, bud. You alright?" Borty also received a heap load of nothing. The quiet was unbearable, but was quickly interrupted by the sound of a hatch slamming open in the corner.

"Fellas. Over here. Look what I found." Turdlet proudly beckoned. When they managed to get a clear view of him, they noticed Turdlet was holding someone. A leprechaun. A hatless leprechaun at that, which meant a luckless one.

"Put me down ye handsy feckless begger," the leprechaun yelled, along with a few creative uses of the word cabbage.

"There's a whole load of stuff like this down here. C'mon!" Turdlet ducked back down into the dark hole, carelessly releasing his fresh catch.

At the bottom of the two-way ladder expanded a jam-packed convention floor.

Crimicon.

Everything they were expecting, there it all was, crammed into a space no taller than four feet. To make up for what it lacked in height, the place stretched out for what seemed like miles.

Humans, eldersnatches, gronks, anything larger than Borty struggled to make their way from stall to stall. There was an extra path installed just for those who need to crawl. The gnomes were in their element. The gnomes could finally see something more than arse and it was beautiful.

The convention centre was lit with donated fairy lights. The fairies, being one of the most popular attractions at the event, had even moved their own hives here for the next few days. Hundreds of thousands of them darted from stall to stall, selling their harvest of liquefied magic for the year. They were like bees to a flower, and puzzle pieces were their nectar. A sweet treat that everyone here had in mind.

"Hey!" grumbled a microtroll. "No weapons in the convention, unless purchased here."

The knobbly-faced creature sat behind a counter by the ladder. She was almost as wide as she was tall. Behind her was a vast array of weapons and potions, many of which the gnomes had never seen before.

"Wow. That's some woman," said Gassy, blushing.

"Uh, well at least she is a woman this time. She's got plenty of...girth," whispered Borty. Girth was an understatement. A microtroll of those proportions only came around once in a generation.

"We'll get them back, right?" asked Turdlet.

"Get what back?" she responded.

"The weapons. Our weapons. We'll get them back."

"Obviously. What do you take me for? I'm an official member of the guild." Accompanying the microtroll's defensive response was her thief's guild ID. It wasn't a flattering picture of her, sketches usually never are, but the gnomes also didn't recall the thief's guild writing their IDs in chalk on the underside of a live beagle.

"Tur...key." Turdlet sounded out as he read the ID's tummy. At the same time, he handed over his entire backpack and his little one-handed crossbow. "Just this, Turkey."

"Your name's Turkey?" Borty emptied his pockets of everything sharp as he stared confused at the microtroll.

"Yes! My name is Turkey. It's a perfectly normal name for a microtroll. It's not strange at all," she said, as her ID began to lick itself.

"I like your name, even if it is stupid," Gassy Bedchambers added.

"Screwoff, the lot of you," demanded Turkey. With a forceful shooing, the gnome gang hurried themselves deeper into the convention.

"I feel like we focused on the wrong detail there," said Gassy.

"More like *she* focused on the wrong detail. Stupid troll. She didn't even check me for explosives," Turdlet quietly boasted.

Immediately alarmed, Gassy asked, "Turdlet. *Should* she have checked you for explosives?"

"Yes. She definitely should have."

"What did Borty say? No unwelcome explosions!"

"I know. It's just my emergency supply."

Borty took a moment separate from the others to be extremely excited before noticing Gassy's growing disappointment. He was dragging his feet and looking down at the floor, mostly due to how carefully you needed to step around the stumpy attendees.

"C'mon, buddy. What's up?" Borty put his arm as far around Gassy as it would go. "You used to love the conventions."

"Yeah. I know."

"So, what's the matter with you? Look, a pocket-sized pony. You love ponies," Borty paused for a moment, "or is it donkeys?"

"It's neither. But I don't like any of this stuff. Everything's all so... small."

"Aha. I get it now."

"I wanted to stand at the bottom of something epic and be like, 'Woah!' But instead it's all pretty mediocre."

"Mediocre? But you're missing the point, Gassy. You see all those army atnits?" Borty pointed to a nearby table, roughly knee height. On the table, a tiny demonstration of military prowess was being performed by a people whose greatest foe was a strong gust of wind.

"Yeah. What about them?"

"Do you have any idea how remarkable you are to those little guys? You live on an island with more storms than there are days and act like it's normal. Storms that would wipe their

72

colonies out in an instant. It took you five minutes to walk from the ladder to over here, but it would take them the better part of a few hours. Gassy, the reason there aren't any impressive sights to see is because, today, you're the marvel of the convention." Borty didn't believe a word of his own bullshit. The atnits weren't stupid either. They know gnomes aren't anything to admire, especially chunky ones with more BO than a jouster's codpiece. But it didn't matter what they thought.

"That's right! I *am* pretty cool, aren't I?" exclaimed Gassy, ignoring his own contradictory knowledge.

"Well, I wouldn't say cool—"

"Dang right, I'm the coolest guy here," continued Gassy. "Nobody is this whole rubbish convention has lived a life as full as mine."

"Let's not get ahead of ourselves." Borty was slowly distancing himself from Gassy.

"C'mon, Borty. Let's not waste any more time." Gassy strode off into the crowds, following a sign directing them to the competition start line.

Keeping his distance, Borty followed behind before noticing something was off, "Gassy, hold-up. Where's Turdlet gone?"

* * * * *

"You're telling me that I don't even have to worry about bugs?" Turdlet feigned excitement.

"That's right sir! The Gangster's Grappling Hook is coated in user-friendly, easy-to-maintain, arsenic preserver. Any bugs that think your grappling-hook looks like a delicious treat will be in for one heck of a surprise." When he finished his sentence, the crowd standing in front of the gobba announcer filled the room with oos and ahhs. A gobba is much like a gnome, only with sharper teeth, pointier ears, and a hairless tail. Unlike gnomes, gobbas are extremely likeable.

"But wait," Turdlet began, "what about my heavier friends? Can the rope really support all of their weight?"

"Of Course! The Gangster's Grappling Hook comes with state-of-the-art arachnofibre roping. Each organically sourced web strand is hand-woven into the strongest rope on the market without the use of dangerous essence-based technology. You couldn't break it, even if you wanted to." More whispers of eagerness came from the crowd, enough to get the attention of Gassy and Borty. As they approached the back of the cheap rabble, they noticed their friend.

"Borty... why is Turdlet on stage?" Turdlet quickly spotted the pair and gave them a suppressed wave.

"I have no idea."

From the extremely short stage, Turdlet locked his eyes on his friends. Borty was miming something with his mouth, but he couldn't tell what. 'W...T...TH...FU...' *A mystery,* thought Turdlet.

"Do you have any more questions?" the announcer cued Turdlet. For a second, he wasn't quite sure what to say. He knew he had to say something.

"Yes. I do."

"Well..." the announcer paused, waiting for a question, "feel free to ask at any time..."

"Uhhh..." the crowd was silent. They were all so immersed in what else the Gangster's Grappling Hook had to offer.

With his impatience, and embarrassment, getting the best of him, the announcer whispered, "demonstr—"

"Ohhh! How about a demonstration then?" Turdlet's delivery of his line was mostly one of satisfaction for remembering what he had been told to say.

"Most certainly, sir! We will be holding a demonstration of this wonderful piece of technology in just a few hours. Be sure to watch the performance, as it will be conducted by none other than the host of Crimicon itself." The announcement from the announcer kicked the crowd into such excitement that they all pushed over each other just for a chance to reach the stage. Everyone wanted one if it was endorsed by the organisers of Crimicon. Little did they know, it wasn't.

Distracted, the announcer didn't even look at Turdlet when he asked, "So, can I get my payment?"

"Sure whatever. Just grab one off the rack," said the gobba.

Giddily, Turdlet rushed over to the rack to pick out his new toy. When the show was clearly over, Borty and Gassy circled around to see their friend carrying a long box on his back. The box barely avoided the ceiling.

"We don't need that, Turdlet. It'll only slow us down," said Borty.

"What d'you mean we don't need it? You don't even know what we're doing for the Crimicompetition yet."

"Look at it. It's huge. How are we going to be inconspicuous with that?"

"This would normally cost two-thousand puzzle pieces, but I got it for free! C'mon, it'll definitely be worth it."

"I have to agree with Turdlet on this one," interjected Gassy, "we don't know our objective yet. It could be really useful."

Borty wasn't one to ignore Gassy's advice when it comes to planning, especially if he was siding with Turdlet. "Alright, fine. You can keep it until the competition is announced, but we're flogging it the moment it sounds like it's going to get in the way."

Turdlet's glee was immeasurable. He was already fantasising about shooting it at just about everything he walked past on their way to the registration line.

Chapter Eight

Chatter filled the competition hall. A hall is one perspective, another would describe it as an old watery cellar with just enough decorations to hide that fact. Even so, the modicum of class it did provide was more than half the crowd had ever seen, and twice as much as three-quarters of them deserved.

Statistically confusing prejudices aside, all eyes were widened with excitement. It was, after all, the first Crimicompetition in years. People dressed in the most criminal outfits they had in their closets. Some dressed as their favourite criminals: Bagman, the Firestoker, and Dr Deciduous (master of horticultural heisting) were among the favourites. Admittedly, the celebrities of the criminal world weren't quite as impressive as its heroic counterparts. Gassy personally believed it was a matter of short lifespan, often arguing that criminals just weren't very good at not dying. A more honest analysis of the situation would show that the main limiter of quality criminals was bad word of mouth.

Criminals just didn't know how to market their brand without getting arrested.

Settled on a few barstools at the back of the room were our chipper little gnomes. They were sipping cups of dragonkeydew (pronounced with the stress on 'gon'). This particular drink was the condensation of the sweat from a fairly common flightless dragon, the sensation of which when drinking could only be likened to having a miniscule cat climb inside your mouth and start boxing your uvula like it was a piñata hiding infinite tummy rubs. Less than pleasant to say the least. However, it was certainly enough to awaken our gnomes after their tediously long queue for entry.

"This is a big turnout," noted Gassy. He wasn't wrong. The audience was close to capacity yet most of those weren't likely to have signed-up for the Crimicompetition. Something still felt off though. A lot of puzzle pieces were being thrown around for a convention underground.

"We've got this," said Borty as if he knew what Gassy was feeling. "This time next year, people will be dressing up as us at Crimicon." Borty then realised he really needed to work on his look, something a little more unique than his standard greased-back-woodsman style. Maybe an accent piece, like a nice blue waistcoat.

"Shhh, it's starting," said Turdlet. Nobody was talking anymore, but he felt the need to shush nonetheless.

The cellar hall (the only part of the convention taller than four feet) had a rather spacious stage at the front. This stage was the only part of the room still lit when the fairy lights dimmed. Quite orderly, the crowd's chatter also dimmed to a whisper. All eyes looked forward in anticipation. They watched nothing.

Suddenly, something.

Another gobba took to the stage dressed in sparkly garb from head to toe. The moment he stepped into the light the crowd burst into a roar of cheers and excitement. The cheers clearly weren't for him, nobody really knew who he was, the cheers were for the moment they were all lost in.

"Welcome back to Crimicon!" the little gobba screamed into the magiphone. He was even more ecstatic than the audience who were practically bent over backwards with ecstasy.

"I love Crimicon," yelled a stranger from the crowd. The gobba pointed with a sleazy smile, as if he knew that person.

"Haha, me too." He'd likely never even been to a Crimicon before, but it didn't stop damn near everyone in the room believing the gobba was one of them. "Thank you so much for waiting. What an immense pleasure it is to be the host for the return of Crimicon. And what a convention this year will be as we introduce to you, what I'm told is, the biggest challenge in Crimicompetition history!" another wave of roars split through the crowd.

"Oh bugger," said Gassy. He sipped more of his dragonkeydew, regretting his sip immediately.

"That's right, we've got some real hush-hush surprises in store for you today. Coming up, we've got a pocket-sized fashion show, an exhibition of what modern magics can do for your personal crime rate, and a whole heap of other exciting events. But, since we're a little late to start, we're kicking things off with something you've all been waiting for..." the room fell dead. Everyone knew what he was going to say but didn't dare celebrate too early. "It's the Crimicompetiooooon!"

The crowd burst into another fit of excitement, even Borty and Turdlet couldn't hold back from getting involved with the cheers. Some attendees were bouncing off the walls in the most literal sense of the phrase.

The gobba host continued, "That's right ladies, gents, and everything in between, thanks to the eagerness of this year's sponsor we're going to start off with our headline event. We have over one hundred applicants for this year's Crimicompetition and boy is this one a doozy. I'm going to get right into it with the category," the gobba waved a shiny envelope in the air. "This year's Crimicompetition's category is... a Treasure Race!"

"Yes!" exclaimed Borty. "First to hand the target in wins. We'll be done with this by the end of the day, boys."

Gassy's reaction wasn't as positive. He ordered another dragonkeydew. He still didn't like it, but Borty had ordered the first round and Gassy didn't know what else was on the menu and wouldn't dream of asking.

"Exciting stuff!" the gobba continued as he swapped to another envelope, "But there's more to come. Let's find out who your target is!"

Hums and whispers waved through the fans as they patiently watched the gobba struggle with his envelope.

"This year's Crimicompetition location is..." he paused. His smile sank into dread. He was reluctant to share his disappointment with the crowd, but it wasn't up to him. "The location is...the manor house of Day Lord. His bedroom to be exact."

The cellar hall became morgue-ish. Decomposing bodies made more noise. Half the crowd thought there must be some mistake, the other half were already considering asking for a refund. Day Lord's manor? They must be insane. The only reason the room remained civil was because Day Lord was on crusade.

"But Day Lord is returning," shouted a random citizen. What remained of the pre-mob's civility was wiped away with those few words. Those competing were backing out of the room to cancel their registration and attendees booed in anger after realising that even most of the criminal world's best would struggle to make it out of this one.

Borty's hype-train immediately felt the brakes of reality. He didn't know how to react. The gnomes already knew how close Day Lord's light strollers were, they'd bumped into them in the woods. There was no arguing it. This was above dangerous.

"That's that then," said Gassy, "I'll go get our refunds."

"No, wait. Let's see what the goal is first," said Borty.

"Trust me, Borty, whatever it is, it's not worth it." Gassy slumped off his chair and started to walk away. Borty grabbed him by the back of his coat and held him in place.

"I said wait."

"For those of you who're still interested, I'll read you the last envelope. The target." The gobba rustled the envelope on stage, rushing as he took notice of how many people were filing out. "This year's target is... the Necrognomicon. If any of you maniacs get it, please follow the Crimicon ribbon to the hand-in location."

Although most of the audience didn't even flinch, Borty and Turdlet perked up right out of their chairs. *That couldn't have been a coincidence*, they collectively thought, *what are the chances of it being that specific target?* Even Gassy couldn't ignore the significance of that book. It was essentially the holy grail of gnome-based relics.

"We're doing it," said Borty.

"I'm all the way in," said Turdlet.

"No. I'm out," said Gassy. He hurried right out the nearest door, along with a good portion of the audience as the gobba tried to introduce the upcoming fashion show.

"Gassy," yelled Borty. He quickly caught up to his chubby companion. "Where're you going? This is our best shot yet."

"Best shot? Are you mad? It's the ruddy Day Lord. That pious prick will eviscerate any 'thief' he finds, which is practically anyone he disagrees with. They'll kill us, Borty."

"Threat of death never stopped us before. Besides, he ain't here yet. It's just his guards, and not even the good ones," said Turdlet.

"Yeah, he'll have taken his light strollers with him on the crusade," added Borty.

"The 'crusade' that happens to be less than a *day* away." Gassy was beginning to be insulted that Borty and Turdlet were even pushing for this. Did they want to die? Did they want *him* to die? Without the proper preparation, Gassy didn't have much chance of staying unscathed in most heists.

"Gassy, we have an advantage that nobody else has. Not to mention, it's a book. You love books," argued Borty.

"My love of books aside, what advantage could we possibly have that would put us ahead of others?"

"We've got the only person still alive that has tried this heist before." Borty and Turdlet looked expectantly at Gassy. His face scrunched up into a frown that gave the appearance of moving his eyes closer to his nose.

"No," he said, definitively.

"Come on, Gassy. You're the only one that can get us into the manor grounds," said Borty.

"Yeah, don't be such a wet nappy," taunted Turdlet.

"Shut up! I'm the only one alive to try it because the last time I did it my entire crew died. I'd be dead too if I hadn't planned such a perfect escape route." Gassy had a momentary flashback of crawling out of one of his crew members, a rotting ooze-ogre, buried in a shallow grave. "There's no way I can escape in one of *your* corpses."

"...Our what?" asked Borty after realising he'd never really gotten the full story on Gassy's previous heist. "Whatever. Your last heist probably failed simply because there were way too many of you. Eleven people on one heist? Ridiculous."

"Don't forget the remaining guards will be distracted by all the other people trying to get in," added Turdlet.

"Exactly!" yelled Borty. "It's practically the perfect conditions. Now's the *only* time we'll have a chance to succeed at this."

Gassy was trying his best to resist Borty's argument without disappointing him, "We can't possibly succeed. We don't even have time to make plans."

"You're just scared," Turdlet laughed until Borty gave him a side glance.

"I'm not scared. I'd just prefer we don't throw our lives away."

Borty could feel Gassy's resistance unravelling, "We don't need plans, bud. Just get us in. Turdlet and I can do the rest. You did it before and that's all you have to do again."

"Oh yeah? And how do you expect me to do that? Just flip you over the—" Gassy stopped himself before he finished his thought.

"And he's in." Borty smiled. He planted his arm around Gassy.

"Yeah alright. I think I know an easy way in." Gassy slumped his shoulders. He loathed himself for giving into these two, but they were going to go anyway. He couldn't let them go without his superior guidance. He quickly grabbed an '(eye) (heart) Crimicon: Under Four Feet' t-shirt for his collection and said, "We better get going then."

Chapter Nine

Gassy stood in front of a seemingly ordinary wall. Resting against it were a few leaky beer barrels and a napping homeless fellow who – considering his current place in life – was rather well-dressed. One of Under-arraz's (sigh) many completely unnecessary laws was all homeless people were expected to wear their best attire at all times, under threat of having their homelessness removed. This law was so badly worded and had so many versions that nobody realised its current state meant any poorly dressed person without a home was entitled to one for free.

"This is the spot," said Gassy. Behind the short wall they could see the top of the manor. The occasional guard helmet bobbed up and down on the roof.

"Are you certain this is the way in?" asked Borty.

"As much as I remember. It'll get us into the grounds at least."

"Good. Turdlet you take the lead for now."

"Are you both sure on the plan?" asked Gassy.

"Of course," said Borty.

"Turdlet?"

"Yeah, I know. We get to the roof with my amazing grappling-hook and take the stairs down from there," Turdlet wasn't even looking at the others, instead he was inspecting the rooftop.

"That's right. No veering from the plan. That staircase is the only bit I can still remember," said Gassy.

"We got it, Gassy. Let's do this." said Borty.

"Are we sure we want to do this?" Gassy hesitated as Turdlet began to climb the barrels. "We hop over this wall and there won't be an easy way back."

"Of course we're doing this. We've been over the plan: We're good. We all know what it's like to be on the losing end of this competition and I'm not about to let that happen again." With a firm stomp of his little foot, Borty rushed over to help Turdlet with his climb.

"I just wanted to be sure." Gassy struggled to climb up the barrels, each one he attempted to mount wobbled as if it was trying to shake him off. He finally found firm footing on one with a little celebration. His minor victory went unseen by Borty who was handing Turdlet his Gangster's Grappling Hook. Turdlet carelessly chucked his new toy over the other side of the wall.

"We'll be right behind you," assured Borty.

With a thud, Turdlet disappeared over the top of the wall. With their vision of him completely obscured, Gassy and Borty were forced to rely on their hearing. It was likely their least exercised sense, since they'd spent years not listening to what other people said. Still, they could hear a rustling from the other side of the wall, but no alarms or sounds of a fight breaking out.

"Fellas. I'm not sure you want to see this," Turdlet choked on his words. He knew his criminal companions would have to follow him, but he so desperately wished to spare their eyes.

"What's wrong? Is it safe?" Borty started to climb up. Even Gassy had managed to lift himself partially up the wall, a feat that resulted in endless jiggling of his cakey behind.

"It's safe. In a way."

"Good enough for me," said Borty, pulling himself over the wall. Safe was a good description. Physically, there were no threats. This was definitely the right spot. No guards, no monsters, nothing to be worried about. But there, pressed up against their landing-pad, was something that threatened to damage more than their bodies. It was a threat to their pride.

"A fucking gnomery."

For the uninitiated, a gnomery is the single most despicable act of prejudice one could perform against a gnome. A gnomery consists of two or more gnome-shaped figures, these figures often finding themselves in silly positions. Depicting a painfully simplified version of gnomes, the gnomery was usually put in the gardens of wealthier people as tacky decorative pieces. On the occasion it might have some deeper meaning to the person, like Dr Biggins three houses down who also installed an enviable gnomery because he was convinced that surrounding his house with statues of thieves would ward off other thieves. His senility prevented him from realising that his horrendous gnomery was helping more gnomes sneak in rather than scare them off. In some cases, it was the only incentive to steal from him.

"This is disgusting," Gassy chimed in. He was rubbing his botty after a less than graceful landing on one of the gnome's fungus-based houses.

"They've made it look like we live in a mushroom. Who do they think we are? Fairies or something?" said Turdlet, in agreement with Gassy for once. This was unacceptable. The sheer size of the gnomery was angering too. It almost stretched the length of a normal house with well over a few dozen statues in increasingly unrealistic poses.

"And look how many of them are women," said Gassy. "Be honest, how many lady gnomes have you ever seen? I can't think of one."

"Exactly! You know what gets me about it most? The hats." Borty's observation roused nods and grumbles from everyone. "Just because one community of gnomes think walking around in big pointy hats is cool, we all have to put up with that offensive depiction."

"It's the worst. Why would you even wear a hat like that? People would see you coming from miles away. You couldn't steal anything," insisted Turdlet.

"It's like they've taken a small subsection of our culture and exaggerated and focused on it to the point that it has becomes an expected trait of our people, thereby lessening any meaningful achievements we've made as individuals as we are forced to be compared to the caricature you see in gnomeries like this one."

...said Gassy.

"How do you ruin the fun in everything we do?" asked Turdlet.

"Hold on a moment. I can be qu—"

"Gassy, shut it!" whispered Borty, loudly. He'd spotted a couple of yard guards walking through the gate into the garden. They each waddled along the garden path, a waddle that made it hard to tell whether their armour was too heavy or they were just too stout for their own good. Even with all the space, there was nowhere to hide. The gnomes would be spotted in seconds.

"Duhnt muhv." Turdlet strained, squeezing out the words without moving his lips. The gnomes froze. Gassy's frown remained plastered to his face.

"...even if I were interested in that sort of thing, with my brother?" said the balder of the two guards.

"Aih do not know why ya put up with'er." The colloquially orientated guard was leaner than his friend. He was also significantly scruffier. His stubble wiggled out of his chin and he sported a rather non-militaristic haircut which wafted the unexpected scent of charcoal.

"Sometimes, neither do I. I should jus'throw her t'the curb, but there's somethin' stoppin' me."

"T'kids?" the scruffier of the two asked, before slowing his footing.

"Nah. Kids're old enough to fend for 'emselves," the bald man began, "Johnathon just turned nine, 'bout time he left the house."

Standing beside the gnomery, the two men stopped for a moment. They inspected the impressive display with worrying frowns of confusion.

"Three new'ns!" announced the leaner guard.

"Why d'they always get new ones without tellin' us?" The balding guard took a step closer to the gnomes. He bent over to their heights and inspected each crack and pimple on Gassy's skin. Gassy held his breath and used every slither of restraint he had to stop from darting his eyes to movement he could see in the corner of his view.

"Don't even 'ave 'ats."

"No hats! Stupid. Wassa gnome without a hat? Nothin'." Turdlet was dreaming of the crossbow on his back as the guards spoke on. Every sentence they said seemed to be seeped in blatant racism. The only thing stopping him from going nuts – other than the immediate threat to their lives – was how ignorant they seemed. They did seem genuinely interested in gnome culture. They'd just been led to believe that this tiny slither of gnome life was gnomality. As he was lost in thought, the guards approached him.

"Hey! Wassis box?" the balding guard asked. He took a knee next to Turdlet and began to open the box beside him when his companion collapsed next to him. "Bloody hells!" he yelled when he noticed his colleague had an arrow halfway through his head.

With seemingly no source of origin, another arrow slung through balding guard's head and disappeared into the distance. The gnomes still didn't budge. They did, however, take a quick peek around them. Dashing out from the shadows were a pair of chameladons. These humanoid reptiles could change not only their appearance but the very structure of their body. They did find limits at about twenty percent volume growth (or shrinkage) but that still allowed them to completely undress the murdered guards and replace their patrol.

Chameladons weren't much to look at, but slithering into that armour and morphing into a 'humanlike' face was far more than just a little unattractive. It was scarring. And the bodies of their victims? What they couldn't eat, the chameladons threw over the wall, spilling all sorts of Day-Lord-knows-what on the still motionless gnomes.

As quickly as they appeared, they were gone.

"Well that was completely fricked," announced Gassy, gagging at his vivid memories. He scrubbed his newly stained clothes with surprising dexterity. The marks were gone in moments. He'd clearly had practice removing stains. Take that as you will.

"They've got a lead on us. Let's kick things up, lads. Who knows who else is ahead of us!" Turdlet tightened his belt and picked up his box, readying himself to rush off.

"We shouldn't rush this. There's no need," said Gassy, "Those are just yard guards. They don't have keys to the manor. Those chameladons still have a lot of work ahead of them to get to the top floor where Day Lord's room should be."

"Even so, Turdlet is right too," began Borty, "caution is good, but we need to hurry."

Chapter Ten

While setting up the Gangster's Grappling Hook, the gnomes had seen at least three other groups trying to get into the manor house from other directions, one of which was immediately shot to pieces by arrows from yard guards. At most sites that would be enough to put the guards on high alert, but it was considered a rather slow day if only one or two people lost their lives trying to get into Day Lord's manor out of desperation.

Aiming the grappling-hook into the sky, Turdlet beamed with excitement.

"This is it boys. Everything we've been working towards for these past few days culminates at this point," said Borty. He began to tear up. "We pull this little trigger and our heist truly begins. Whatever happens from now, I want you to know I really appreciate what you've put up with to get to this point."

Gassy whimpered, "You can always rely on us, Borty."

Turdlet was shaking with anticipation, his fist clenched in front of him ready to cheer.

"Alright. Go for it." Borty winced.

Turdlet pulled the trigger. The long, spear-like hook launched from its barrel with a rope attached to one end. In the blink of an eye, the projectile was gone. To the dismay of the group, the rope was very much still present. In fact, it had launched a very short distance before reaching its end and becoming untangled from the hook.

"Oh. Oh dear. Of course. Under four feet. I suppose that applies to the rope too," said Borty.

"Why did none of us think to test it first?" asked Gassy. Turdlet seemed to be the only one not disappointed, still frozen with his excited look waiting for something to happen.

In that very moment, a series of miraculous coincidences all converged at once. You see, earlier in the day, the manor's cook badly injured her hand, while shopping for ingredients, in a small scuffle between a mob (she was a part of) and an extremely disrespectful young guard. And so, her rather inexperienced daughter, Josi, was forced to fill in for her mother from fear of losing such a well-paid job. Much to the surprise of the other kitchen staff, Josi performed both admirably and diligently. Her handmade strawberry trifle was particularly in high demand, a fact the innocent young woman put down to the love she instilled in her desserts. In reality, Josi had mistaken the chef's personal 'energy salts' as sugar – a mistake that anyone with experience in a professional kitchen would know to look out for – and had unknowingly been dosing the members of the household.

Due to the quick popularity of her trifles, the Head Guard himself insisted on the finest trifle she could muster. Recalling a tale earlier in the month from her mother talking about how much of a sweet-tooth the Head Guard had, Josi knew to add a whole spoonful of extra 'sugar'. Again, completely unaware of its effects, Josi proudly presented her finest creation to the Head Guard. He gleamed with utter satisfaction as the pudding went down a treat. Unfortunately for him, only a few minutes back on patrol and he began to feel the hallucinogenic effects of a bad dosage from this drug. He wondered aimlessly around the manor giving nonsense orders until the effects began to wear off. As lucidity started to return, his immediate thought was to rush to the roof to take in some fresh air. That'd clean his system out. So that's what he did. There, on the precipice of the tallest building in town, the Head Guard enjoyed the calm of comfortably coming down. This calm was cut brief, however, by a four-foot projectile piercing through his chest and launching him up into the air. The last thoughts to run through his head as he hurtled back down to the ground were as follows: *I hope I land on that fat little gnome.*

"Bloody hells!" yelled Borty as he tackled Gassy. A split second later, the corpse of an oddly disappointed guard landed beside the group.

"Yay! Great success!" screeched Turdlet as he nabbed the dozens of keys from the guard's side. "Oh look, he brought the grappling-hook back too. We can try shooting it again."

"No! We're not doing that again. This is bad, very bad," insisted Gassy.

"It's fine. There's a service door around here, right? We've got some keys now. We'll just get in that way," said Borty.

"That's not part of the plan. None of this is part of the plan," declared Gassy as he gestured to the crumpled Head Guard's corpse.

"You're only scared because you know you couldn't handle a fight," taunted Turdlet.

"I'm not scared. Borty, you know that the moment things start to go bad, we need to think of a way out. This is it. This is the start of things going bad."

Borty looked around as he crafted his response. "This isn't bad. We quite literally have the keys to the castle—"

"It's a manor," added Turdlet.

"Yes, thank you, Turdlet." Borty took the new keys and placed them in Gassy's hands. "We should easily be able to get to the top floor with these. All we have to do is sneak past the guards and get to Day Lord's room before he arrives and—"

"Look!" interrupted Turdlet. "The building across the way."

He pointed at the roof of the building opposite Day Lord's keep. Just barely visible through the ribbons, the gnomes spotted a MagInc portable ski-lift – trademark pending. It hadn't started moving yet, but was being loaded with what looked like a half-dozen armed thieves.

"It's Breezy! That arrogant arsehole is going in wands a'blazing," barked Borty. "He's going to get there first! Doubletime, boys."

"But the plan..." said Gassy.

"We still have a plan, Gassy. It's just a new one." Borty reached out his hand. Gassy gave in, but he didn't take the hand.

Turdlet joined the others as they rushed-off, but he didn't forget to take a moment to lament leaving his grappling-hook behind.

* * * * *

Just a few hops out of the vegetable garden and they were by the service entrance. Their eyes on the sky, they almost didn't notice the greeting of a porter on his smoke break.

"Alright fellas?" asked the slender staffman. He certainly wasn't all human, but there was at least a little in him. A mix of some sort. Far from pedigree mind you, which made him nearly as disliked as a gnome.

"Alright?" Turdlet answered with his own rhetorical question. "Lovely weather today we're having."

"Ooo yeah, lovely. First spot of sunshine in a few days now." the porter smiled as Borty and the boys started walking up the steps.

"Let's hope it lasts, eh?"

"Haha, it never does, does it?" the porter seemed happy just to have someone to talk to. As Turdlet's perfectly pedestrian conversation continued, Gassy fumbled for the service door key. "You lads new here then? What've they got you doin'?"

"Err..." Turdlet started, he hadn't thought this far ahead. He rarely did.

"Shit shovelling duty," said Borty.

"Shit shovellin'?" the porter repeated in disbelief. "What happened to Bert? He's shovelled here for almost ten years now."

"Well, with Day Lord coming, they figured he might need a few pairs of extra hands in his old age."

"But Bert only turned fifteen last week." The porter stated. As Borty bartered for time, Gassy shuffled through the keys, struggling to find the right one.

"Getting on then. Most shovellers don't make it out of their teens."

"Flipping heck! I didn't realise it was such a dangerous job. I guess that explains why they'd hire gnomes." The porter had a sudden epiphany of gratefulness for his laid-back occupation.

Brushing over the porter's ignorant comment, Borty continued, "Ohhh yeah. It's *very* dangerous. One in three shovellers die before their sixth birthday. Contagious too, if you get too close. Best keep your distance." He slowly stepped backwards after hearing the click of the lock.

"That's dreadful. If only there was a way to move your crap around a house without using a shovel. Something that's a little more hands-off." The porter was tearing up at the thought of such tragic loss.

"Unfortunately, there isn't. I guess for now it's just a pipe dream." Borty smiled as he started to close the door behind him.

"A what?" the gnomes were already gone before the porter got an answer.

On the other side of the door was a quiet mini-foyer with no one in sight.

"Next time we need to open a door in a hurry, let's not give the keys to potato fingers over here," said Turdlet, snatching the keys from Gassy.

Hurt, and a little self-conscious about his tubby tuber fingers, Gassy looked to Borty. "How do you know so much about shovelling poop?"

"Well, you have to know these things when you're a thief, you know." Borty insisted as he led the way into the manor.

What Borty didn't let Gassy know is just how much of what he said was completely made up. For example, one in three shovellers did not die before their *sixth* birthday, but before their *ninth*.

Chapter Eleven

Day Lord's kitchen wasn't nearly as big or as fancy as the gnomes had expected. Even Gassy hadn't been here before. It was still about the size of your average family's hovel, but there were far fewer people rushing about here than there was outside, or even in said family hovel.

"Hellooo," said Josi with a pleased smile on her face. She brushed the loose ends of her plaited hair behind her shoulder with the back of her powdery hands. "I'm Josi. I'm new."

Josi was older than her unjaded spirit presented. In most families, particularly the affluent ones, Josi would already be married with a child well on the way by now. Perhaps she'd be running her own little venture or finishing her last year in higher education. Essentially, she was old enough for it to not be weird that Gassy had stopped dead in his tracks. He was stunned. She had stunned him.

"Hello Josi, we're actually also new. We've been hired as temporary staff." Borty stepped in with a charming smile.

"Oh yes, for Day Lord. My mum has been looking forward to seeing him again all week," she said, looking a little saddened. "She's never had a chance to meet him yet but is so excited at the idea. I do hope it happens soon."

Suddenly, as if whatever had jammed his gears unclogged itself, Gassy spoke up, "Hello! I'm Gassy."

His stiff eagerness would have likely scared-off most, but not Josi. She responded with a smile, "Nice to meet you, Gassy. Would you care for a strawberry trifle?"

"Yes," yelled Gassy without missing a beat. He immediately dug into his delicious dessert.

"No, thank you," said Borty, looking uncomfortable next to Gassy's eating habits. Turdlet also shook his head, instead opting for inspecting the nearby hallway. "Say, Josi?"

"Yeah?"

"You don't happen to know how many guards are in the building today?"

"Of course I do! There's at least sixty inside, and they're all so hungry," Josi blurted out a goofy laugh that fondly reminded Borty of donkeys. Mimicking her, Gassy also gave a less endearing chortle.

"Cun uh huv anuvuh?" asked Gassy, spraying most of what was left of his trifle on the table in front of him.

"You most certainly can!" she declared. Every desperate bite Gassy took added a new smile-crinkle on her face. She'd been receiving praise all day but none as so vulgarly honest as his. Her fondness for gluttons was built into her from a younger age. Josi used to hand out her mother's cup-pies – pies shaped like half-pint tankards – and any time she saw a heavier-set man, she knew he'd buy several from her. Almost all of her regular customers were at least chunky. They were also the people that supported her family through some truly hard times. Some of those hard times were happening in that very moment as her father rested at home after a set of floorboards gave out under his remarkable weight and he broke both of his ankles.

No, even though life could be difficult at times, Josi had never once experienced the depravity of man. A cosy layer of affection somehow always protected her from the deplorables of the world and their many conniving ways, so at no point in her life had she ever thought to be distrustful of someone.

"Sixty, huh? That's quite a lot of guards," began Borty, "I don't suppose you know a nice quiet way around them? We want to disturb as few people as possible."

Eager to be useful, Josi jumped in with what knowledge she had, "I definitely know a few ways. But like I said, I'm pretty new. Where are you trying to get to?"

"I thought we'd work our way from the top down."

"Well, you have to start somewhere," she smiled. Gassy smiled too, even though he hadn't been able to focus on the conversation for a while now. He was feeling...different.

"Borty," said Turdlet. He made a few seemingly meaningless gestures that Borty quickly translated as hurry up.

"I think your best route would be to take the service steps just on the other side of the hallway. They're pretty narrow so the guards don't like to use them anyway. I imagine all that armour gets in the way." Her sentence was topped with yet another goofy laugh.

"Thank you Josi, you've really helped us out." Josi shared one last satisfied smile with Gassy as she watched him get dragged away by the others gnomes.

* * * * *

The skip over the hallway was easy enough. There were indeed guards, but they were so abuzz with excitement for Day Lord's return that their awareness wasn't quite what it should be. The gnomes hurried up the service stairs, a spiral set that would certainly be quite tight for any human. Everything was running quite smoothly. It was probably the easiest heist they'd ever participated in. Yet, something felt off to Borty. Once they reached the top, Borty stood on the other side of the door, halting their advance.

"Listen," he said, "you two need to get yourselves together."

"What?" said Gassy. His mind was a little fuzzy right now, but he thought he was doing a good job so far. What about him needed to be gathered?

"Up until this floor, we probably could have talked our way out of things, but we go through this door and we *will* be killed. They find us, we die. It's that simple. You get distracted, or wander off, or think with anything other than your heads, then we're dead." Borty rubbed his forehead. He struggled to look his biggest fan in the eye. Expecting no response from the group, Borty readied himself to open the door. With his hand on the handle, he was interrupted.

"You're not all that either," said Gassy.

"What was that?"

"Yeah. You brought us together for this competition, knowing full well I rely on a solid plan, and then you threw us into a heist and abandoned any preparations we had *immediately.*" Gassy was making gestures with his hands on almost every syllable, an action completely out of his control.

"That's the nature of the competition, bud. We didn't know what the goal was until they told us then and there. Are you telling me you would be happier if it wasn't a race?"

"No. A race is fine." Every word Gassy said looked like a revelation on his face. Like he was learning as he spoke. "We didn't know what it was going to be but you still could have prepared something. Anything. But you just made us think it would be okay. You keep acting like it's all going to be okay."

"Isn't it okay? Look where we are. In fact, if you didn't conveniently forget this place's layout, we could have walked all the way to Day Lord's room." Borty's voice was bouncing between a yell and a whisper.

"Trauma has a funny way of making you forget things, yet I still got us inside the walls. What have you done for us? Even Turdlet brought the grappling-hook that got us the keys. All you've done so far is talk about poop. Josi was more useful than you." Gassy was as surprised at his outburst as Borty was. It wasn't the time, or the place, but he seemed adamant to air his thoughts. "And another thing, you act like you're all cool and like you could talk your way out of anything. You can't. I don't know if you've noticed or not, but people tend not to like us. It's not because we're gnomes either, it's earned. We're awful."

There was a long uncomfortable pause. In the quiet, the gnomes could hear a pair of guards march past the door. Below them, they could hear the growing chatter of people coming up the stairs.

"Now's the time to go, boys," said Turdlet. He wasn't much fazed by the argument since it wasn't directed at him. "Day Lord could be coming any moment. Let's wrap this drama up."

Reluctantly, they both agreed to give up on the conversation. Borty, Gassy, and Turdlet zipped out of the door and under a nearby table.

Gassy began to slowly recall just how busy the halls were with decorative or gifted furniture. His memories were reinforced when spotting the occasional piece of armour or painting from cultures and countries half a continent away. The table they huddled under, for example, was made from deadwood from the Backlybonpa tribe. The Backlybonpa's odd obsession with metal weapons had become so ingrained in their culture that even the table – which was mostly made of wood – was designed like a sword. In cases of bestowing a great honour, they made the effort to hide blades in the undersides of tables to protect against betrayals and home invasions of which there were many in Backlybonpa society. This particular table, noted Gassy, did not have a hidden weapon. Not even a hint of one.

Further mental notes from Gassy pointed to a good number of cultural faux pas adorning the walls down the corridor. He didn't recognise a lot, but he did know enough to realise that many of the decorations were intentional insults that had clearly gone amiss.

"People really hate this guy," said Gassy.

"That's because he's a self-righteous tyrant that forces his beliefs onto others. Now if we don't hurry up, he'll force his beliefs onto us too, over and over again until we're a red mist. So, which way?" Borty asked himself. He didn't look to Gassy, instead trying to solve the problem on his own from his little squatting position. When the silence didn't reveal the answer to his question, Gassy decided he would take a swing at it.

"Straight ahead," he said.

"Why?" questioned Borty.

"Because, his whole shtick is sun-based. That's his sigil, right? Straight ahead should be the east side of the building. If his room is going to be anywhere, it's there."

A little reluctant to accept that Gassy was right, Borty ran his fingers along the engravings of the table as he explored his surroundings. A patrol popped out the door the gnomes had dived from. Gassy froze as the guards walked away, immersed in a heated debate about the importance of soap when cleaning between your toes. When the gnomes were sure they were gone, they shuffled out of their hiding spot and walked down the corridor.

At the end of the corridor, they reached a T-junction. Directly ahead was a door. They froze.

"Which way?" asked Borty, swallowing his pride again.

"I don't know. We need to go east," said Gassy.

"Yeah, we did that. Now what? Is it behind this door?"

"No, I don't think so. The building is much longer than just one corridor in length. This would have been a lot easier if we entered on the right side of the building." Gassy's tone changed to that of a teenager mocking his parents who can't keep with the times. A sort of naïve know-it-allness.

"Well, we didn't. This is where we are so—" before Borty could finish his thought, they heard the gentle clattering of heavy armour to their right.

"Hello?" a phantom voice called. As if rehearsed a thousand times before, the gnomes dived into hiding spots with remarkable professionalism: Gassy found himself under another Backlybonpa table, Borty hid inside a good old-fashioned torturecophagus (like an iron maiden but much prettier), and Turdlet dug his daggers into the wall and hung himself up just above the table as if displaying some game.

A second guard called out.

"Who's there?" he said. They both unsurely crept around the corner to inspect the corridor.

"I hate old buildings like this. There're so spooky. Why can't we just go back to guarding camps or walls like we normally do?" the younger of the guards feigned inspection as the other looked solemnly ahead.

"Because we have our orders. We take those orders and fulfil them with gratitude." He was much surer with his stance, and significantly older. The younger guard looked to his senior with expectedness. He did his best to follow his lead, exploring his surroundings with forced effort before his eyes landed on Turdlet.

"Bloody hells!" he gagged as he yelled. "That's morbid. Who would hang that up on the wall?"

"Don't be disrespectful," the older guard demanded, clapping his junior upside the helmet. "People as powerful as Day Lord wouldn't hang just anyone on his wall. This must have been a truly powerful foe. A point of pride. And right outside his dining hall. He holds this ugly gnome with great respect."

"But it'll rot just hanging here like this."

"It's magic, my friend," he conveniently explained. "Magic can preserve anything in such perfect condition that it looks like it's alive. Especially Day Lord's. Watch." The older guard drew his blade with unwavering confidence.

"Wait, what are you doing?"

"Observe. I can run him through, and this incredible spell will repair his wounds in an instant." The guard prepared his lunge with an unusual eagerness. The gnomes sat in their hidey-holes just hoping this moment would pass, but they couldn't sit by any longer. Gassy had already discovered a hidden Backlybonpa blade which he immediately used to parry the guard's thrust. He almost ran into the blade itself which didn't even faze him, completely separate from Gassy's usual cowardliness. In the exact same beat, Turdlet hopped off his anchor point, taking his daggers with him, and used Gassy as a stepping-stone to reach the older guard where he plunged said daggers into the crooks of his armour. Blood spurted everywhere. It gushed with such force that everyone could taste metal within seconds. Thank goodness there were no carpets.

The younger guard watched this unfold with horror. He struggled to draw his blade. Even when he was wielding it, he was in such a blind panic that his weaponry simply bounced off his own comrade's armour. Swing after swing, he failed to hit Turdlet. Tears overtook him. He was preparing to run. Taking advantage of the distraction, Borty rushed the younger fellow from behind. Although, there wasn't nearly as much joy in his face as there was on Turdlet's, Borty forced his shortsword into the back of the guard's knee. To the surprise of everyone, the younger man flung himself backwards with a blood-curdling scream. The scream was cut short as he cracked his neck on the corner of the torturecophagus.

The older guard continued his struggle. As strength sapped from him, he tried to snuff Turdlet out. He choked the little gnome. His struggles turned to whimpers as he realised he no longer had the strength left to hurt his attacker. This seeping strength soon decided he could no longer stand. Then, he could no longer hold his hands up. Finally, he no longer had the strength to continue breathing.

The gnomes stood in the silence of the room for a moment. Blood was all over the place. The walls, the floor, the lovely decorations. Gassy laid his new weapon on the table as he struggled to lift it above his head.

"This is fricked," said Gassy. "Another guard could find this any minute." Gassy looked at Borty. He didn't have anything smart to say, or any suggestions that might fix this. Nothing short of a mop and a pack of wild dogs would clean this mess up.

"Now what?" asked Turdlet.

"Good question. We should be able to get out the way we came."

"No," said Borty. He didn't look at the others. "We aren't going yet. We're so close." His eyes were desperate. It was clear the only way he would be going is forward.

"But we can't just keep going," argued Gassy, "this is what's wrong with not planning! We now have two pretty messy bodies and no idea where to go or even a plan for escape."

"It's royally borked," added Turdlet.

"Guys," Borty sighed, "how many missions, how many heists, how many times have we been in situations like this?" He paused to give them a chance to respond. His questions were met with silence. Not a good silence. The quiet was quickly broken.

"Exactly! We *always* get into stupid trouble like this. That's it, after this, I'm not doing another heist without a clear, thought through plan." Gassy crossed his arms.

"How many times have we gotten out of situations like this?" Borty waited in yet more silence, this time without a rebuttal. Gassy wanted to speak, but he didn't have a good comeback for that one. They knew how much Borty had done for them, in the bigger picture. He'd discovered them.

He was the one that brought them together. They had achieved a lot, and failed a lot, but it was always together, thanks to Borty. Time with Borty was an adventure... and adventure was dangerous.

Gassy shrugged his shoulders as he looked around.

"It doesn't matter to me, either way. Can we just stop fighting over this?" Turdlet cleaned his blade, and sheathed it, waiting for someone to give in.

"Fine. Say we keep going, what do you expect us to do?" asked Gassy.

"We hide the bodies, and hurry our arses up. We still have time before Day Lord arrives." With no more hesitation, the others were on board. They owed him this one.

Chapter Twelve

Day Lord's upstairs dining hall was more lavish than any other room the gnomes had seen so far, which admittedly wasn't many. Even though it was the top floor, the room was clearly two stories tall which meant it protruded out onto the roof. This explained why half of the room's space was taken up by a grandiose, bifurcated staircase that split towards the east and the west. When first peeking at the enormous room, Borty had expected to see a guard, or two, half-asleep as they stood watch. Surprisingly, there was nobody. The room was instead filled with paintings on every inch of the wall and one long table. One side of the room was completely windows, which made a lovely pairing with the contrastingly modest skylight.

Gassy recognised the room, but his body was distracting him from recovering his memories with flushes and hot sweats.

After dumping the new bodies in one of the many culturally sensitive trunks out in the hallway, the gnomes wanted desperately to dash through this room. However, considering this place was the centre of the building, a wall of windows proved an unwelcome surprise, especially since it faced a courtyard that could have any number of eyes. Instead of creating quick, scuttering movements that might catch the eye of a half-attentive guard, Turdlet led the way in his self-developed slithering motion. The style consisted of a series of unnoticeable movements that resulted in the user lying on their belly performing some sort of elaborate sidewinder motion. It was a tried-and-undertested technique that Turdlet used all the time, you just haven't noticed until now. That's how good it is. Having said that, Turdlet's moves were harder to follow for some more than others.

At the back, wondering what got him to this point in his life, Gassy wobbled his already exhausted, increasingly slippery body along the floor. His movements were less like a sidewinder and more like a walrus. This was also where he realised his shirt was a little too short for him as all the gnomes could hear was the slapping of his muffin-top clapping against the cool wooden floor. As if alarmed by this sound, Gassy's blubbery noise was suddenly replaced by the crashing of armour thundering down the stairs.

"It's the guards, hide!" whisper-shouted Borty.

Gassy peeled himself off the floor in a panic and rushed around in circles, along with his friends, to realise there was nowhere to hide. The only decorations this place had were paintings and the table didn't even have a table-cloth which frankly sickened Gassy. What of the water rings?

With no choice left, the gnomes pressed themselves against the split of the stairs.

The crashing of the armour didn't seem to slow. Whoever it was seemed to be moving quite fast. The gnomes looked at each other with worry. Anyone moving that fast in amour was someone to be afraid of. Then, as if to put their hearts at ease, the bannisters above their heads gave way to the bodies of two heavily armoured guards. They split right through the carefully carved wood and gained a little air before settling on top of the sturdy table. There was a brief pause. Silence sat in the air as splinters found their way to the floor.

"You *idiots*!" barked a familiar voice. The gnomes' fear was instantly halted. They stood up and looked at each other with the same manner of 'well don't we feel stupid'.

"You said take care of'em. They're taken care of," a rather irritated voice responded.

"*Take care* implies you quietly deal with them, not throw their corpses down a staircase where anybody could be stood." The voice and its little feet reached the split in the staircase with a stroppy little stomp.

"But ya said this room was s'pposed to be empty."

117

"That does not mean it *will* be empty. Not everything is as empty as your head." The little footsteps hurried towards the eastern door when Borty decided it was time to make their presence known.

"Hello, Breezy. Always a pleasure."

Breezy shivered like he'd seen someone biting their spoon while eating soup, like only a soulless monster would. "Why are you here?" he said. "Sorry, correction, how are you here?"

"Anything you can do, we can do gooder," said Turdlet.

As Breezy turned to face them, his four other shrouded colleagues stood behind him. "Your words pain me, Turdlet. It is almost as painful as your attempts. You know you cannot win. You have never even come close."

"Neither have you," said Borty, "I don't even think you placed in the last competition."

"That was not fair," yelled Breezy, "nobody won that year, not after that nightmarish tragedy. The bottles were all anyone could think of." A silence fell in the air as everyone paid their respects to something that scarred them all in some way.

"You're headed east, aren't you?" said Gassy, triumphantly. "That's where his bedroom is. That's where the book is."

"It does not matter where the book is. You will not be seeing it." Breezy pulled out his 'essence catalyst' and brandished it in front of him, much to the dismay of his followers.

"Bre..." one began before receiving a cold look, "Boss. Let's just leave'em here. They aren't gunna overpower us and you said to not make a noise. Makes a lotta noise them...es...essem...not-wands."

"We are going to put a stop to them, right now."

"But Day Lord could be 'ere any minute. We should ge'a move on."

"No!" barked Breezy. "You do not know them like I do. They are little beasts in disguise. Not even gnomes, really. We leave them alone and they will find a way to ruin everything we have put together. Borty and Turdlet are bad enough on their own but together they somehow manage to foil any of my plans while simultaneously failing their own."

"Woah!" said Borty, shocked at how offended he was.

"That's mad. Can't believe you think we ever plan anything to begin with," added Turdlet.

"*I* plan things. It's not easy to make a solid plan with you two on my team," said Gassy.

"Thank you, Gassy!" Breezy gestured to his tubby equal with pride. "I just cannot understand what you see in these fools. Think of what remarkable plans we could actually implement. You would not have to deal with their unpredictability. Instead, everything could go according to plan."

"Well, they're not all ba—"

"Do not let them trick you into thinking they are worth your time. What do they truly offer you but pain and hardship? I know what it is like, Gassy, I have worked with them before as well. They are irresponsible and even destructive. They are just holding you back from realising your potential. Join our team, Gassy. As a welcome gift, I will split my share of the reward."

Gassy inspected his gnomemates. The offer was tempting. They did definitely mess up most of his plans, whether they meant to or not. Turdlet stared at Gassy, silently begging him to leave. Borty turned his head away from Gassy. He didn't argue. He didn't bargain. He only seemed to present guilt. Gassy didn't expect that. He didn't expect most of what Borty and Turdlet did. Of what his friends did (although that term was loosely used where Turdlet was concerned).

"No thank you," said Gassy.

"What?" said Breezy.

"I said, no thank you."

"Do not just say no. Think about it for a moment. Think about what you are turning down here. I will not present this offer again. You can work with MagInc. *MagInc!* Everything they plan comes together in the end, even you buffoons cannot avoid that."

"I understand, but I'd rather not. You see, as much as I do like my plans, not everything runs according to them. Sometimes in life your plans just don't happen the way you expect. Things change. It's important to change with them. To adapt to the unpredictability. That's something I've never been very good at, but I don't need to be, because I have these guys to do that for me."

As if he were cued for the perfect ambush, Turdlet grabbed the nearest painting off the wall and cracked it over Breezy's head. Although it didn't have much effect on Breezy's wellbeing, it caused his reflexed blast of energy from his 'not-wand' to shoot straight into the floor with a glorious crackle.

"If they didn't know we were here before, they do now," announced Borty as Gassy planted a rather peaceful landscape over one of the other's head. The gnomes tried to quickly slip by their opponents but when another deadly blast of energy shot past Turdlet, searing the edge of his arm, it was clear getting away wouldn't be easy. There was only one option. More paintings.

The gnomes worked together, splitting frame and canvas over the heads of their five aggressors. They each dodged and weaved around the raw 'essence'. Their years of practice evading rotten vegetables and anger-soaked bottles were finally being put to good use.

Zaps and crackles filled the dining hall. Borty ducked out of danger, countering with the corner of a canvas. Turdlet finally put his little crossbow to good use, hitting his opponents more than once. Breezy panicked. This wasn't part of his plan. Gassy, on the other hand, followed Borty's lead. He mimicked every move Borty made (with much less success) until the gnomes had completely dispatched of Breezy's crew. Bruised, battered, and badly burned, they looked to Breezy.

"Stay back!" he yelled. He brandished his not-wand at the gnomes as one of his companions slowly suffered from one of Turdlet's knives sticking out of his chest.

"It's over Breezy. You've given us away. In just a few moments, guards will come crashing through this door." Gassy pointed to the eastern door. His tone was seeped in pity. "Put down your... essence catalyst, and we might just be able to get out of this one yet."

Breezy paused. He stared at Gassy. "I *am* getting out of here with the book. I will just blast the guards away too, after I have blasted you," for a flashing second, Breezy pointed his weapon at the door. Without a moment of hesitation, he was knocked onto his arse by a flying piece of ornate portrait frame. It happened so quickly that he didn't even see who threw it. His weapon skittered across the floor and, in the same breath, his hand was cuffed to the nearest stair bannister.

"I knew these would come in handy!" exclaimed Turdlet. Breezy kicked and screamed as he reached for his 'essence catalyst' but Borty pocketed it before Breezy could grasp it. In a moment of pure rage, Breezy yanked the dagger from his companion's chest and slashed through the air. Gassy caught the sharp end of it with his leg. Thankfully for him, Breezy's positioning didn't allow for much force, but the blade still pierced right across the top layer of his thigh.

"OOO RUDDY BISCUIT!" capitalised Gassy as he hopped around holding his leg.

"Hold still," commanded Borty, rushing over to inspect the wound. He slowly removed the dagger, chucking it to the ground. Blood seeped out, but its flow was slow.

"How is it?" Gassy asked, looking up to the ceiling in fear of the damage he'd just taken. He couldn't feel it though. He actually still felt great, if a little sweaty.

"It's not too bad. But we don't have a regeneration remedy. We need to move. Now." Borty was kind. He didn't want to scare Gassy. The damage truly wasn't serious, but he knew just how much this could slow them all down.

The gnomes hurried to the eastern door. Breezy called out to them, "You would not dare just leave me here."

They dared.

* * * * *

By this point, it's safe to say we're about two-thirds of the way through our little story. A story that, so far, has done its very best to stay grounded in what might be considered a rather shaky foundation. Positively wobbly, even. What foundation is that? You may ask yourself.

The gnomes, of course.

As I hope you've picked up on by now, Turdlet, Gassy, and Borty aren't the most heroic of heroes. They rarely did anything worth doing, and the things they did, did little for those they were doing them for, if in fact they did anything for anyone other than themselves.

Heroic is likely one of the few descriptors that applied the least to the gnomes, unless you mistake that same descriptor to mean a bipedal humanoid with a level of sleuthability that a sociopathic raccoon would envy.

That's how it's been their whole lives.

Even their most 'heroic' of members, Borty, hardly did anything brave worth mentioning – although it *is* worth noting that Gassy would argue Borty's ability to hold a meaningful conversation a bravery in and of itself. Some might say Turdlet was often brave, but he was just a special kind of destructive. Turdlet would regularly say Gassy's ability to not want to throw himself off a bridge was also brave, even if Turdlet didn't really feel that way.

No, the gnomes were never much bothered with being heroic. Why would they be?

They had no role model in their younger years to aspire towards. No saviours in capes. No god-heroes with a fascination for woodworking tools. No country-based supergnomes wielding a pan lid.

Just suddenly, life.

For those of you unfamiliar with life, it can be awfully unforgiving and downright contemptable at times. The harder it is, the harder you become, and boy has life been particularly rough on our gnomes.

That's why, when an act of true heroism and selflessness is committed by someone from such beginnings, it's that much more remarkable.

Chapter Thirteen

"Borty?" said Gassy. Leaving the dining room was far less appealing now that they saw what lay behind the eastern door. "What's our move here?"

To their left and right, the gnomes discovered a whole entourage of guards. Maybe a half dozen with more rustling down the corridor. Everyone was still. It was a particularly unique situation for the guards. They hadn't quite trained for the moment when thieves and vandals would present themselves so perfectly for capture. The gnomes, on the other hand, were afraid to make any sudden movements. *Perhaps they haven't seen us*, thought Turdlet.

"Hey," said a confused guard, "you aren't supposed to be here."

As if the words were a spell to incite chaos, every guard burst into pursuit of the gnomes who whizzed away down the corridor ahead of them. Borty and Turdlet steamed ahead. Where their little legs would usually fail in a sprint, their

126

pursuers were weighed down by their incredibly ornate armour.

"Just get to the door," cried Borty, "we get inside and reassess."

"Slow down guys," called Gassy. Borty turned to see his portly amigo struggling to keep up. Even on a good day Gassy wasn't much of an athlete but it was clear his little wound was keeping him from reaching his rather disappointing potential. Suddenly, one of the nimbler guards tackled Gassy. They were barely halfway down the corridor when a pile-up began. Guard after guard thought the best choice was to pile onto Gassy instead of continuing pursuit.

Borty had to make a choice. Their goal was ahead, but behind him was his friend who had now disappeared under bumbling bodies.

What can I do? He thought, as he realised the number of guards had doubled. *He's lost.*

Borty turned away. He continued his run down the corridor when something stopped him. In the chaos of clattering armour, Borty could hear a whisper of a cry, "Borty, help me!"

He couldn't keep going. He had to go back. But what could he do? Borty pulled the weapon – which was absolutely a wand – from his pocket. He didn't have any magical knowledge. Any talent in the way of 'essence'. The glowing stick beckoned to him as the crying voice faded in the crowd. He made a decision. It didn't matter if he could

127

use the absolutely-a-wand or not, he was even more unlikely to leave his friend behind (on second thought, at least). He stuck his new weapon out ahead of him and charged towards the pile, as if he were a jouster aiming his lance. He screamed an 'unpractised' war cry. The closer he got, the more he feared for his friend. Suddenly, with a flash of blue light, the absolutely-a-wand flung the pile of testosterone down the corridor. Gassy was revealed, bruised but alive, and almost as surprised as Borty.

"Here, take this," said Borty, handing Gassy the absolutely-a-wand as he gave him a piggy back.

"You came back!" Gassy gleamed, taking the weapon in his hand.

"Yeah, let's not dwell on it." Borty hastened down the corridor, but the guards were hot on his heels. As impressive and impactful as his blast was, it didn't even scuff their amour. However, with Gassy at the helm, his little stick of power penetrated through everyone that got too close. Little zaps of green energy de-legged or de-necked their pursuers. He'd gotten through five of them before turning back to Borty.

"Battery's dead," he said, throwing it to the ground.

"Turdlet, that door better be open when we get there!" yelled Borty. The whole time Gassy lagged behind, Turdlet was working his way into the remarkably complicated lock that this door held. It clearly wasn't complicated enough, as the click of victory allowed him to ease open the door.

"I really hope this is the right room!" said Gassy as they ran through the open door. Turdlet slammed it behind them, locking it from the inside. A second later, the crash of armour could be heard against it.

They were finally safe...for now.

"This is *definitely* the room," Borty declared. He said it with such confidence for one main reason: it was filled with sunlight.

They found themselves in a dome-shaped room of glass with a view of the horizon, on all sides but the west. The first few feet of the glass dome were opaque, likely for structural reasons, and just about reached the height of the bed that lay in the centre of the room.

At the end of the bed was an incredibly expensive looking trunk. The kind that, if they could take it with them, would set the gnomes up for life and then some. Thieving is difficult to make a living from but it's even harder when your little hands can't run off with anything more cumbersome than a watermelon. And don't get me going on the other elemental types of melons. A firemelon is a nonstarter.

"Check the chest. The guards aren't getting through that reinforced door without a key. Turdlet, keep us posted," commanded Borty. The guards banged from the other side without any sign of making it through.

Gassy hobbled over to the chest on his good leg. Borty inspected their surroundings. He couldn't see an escape. There were windows, but the opaque part of the wall blocked his view of any possible climb down. He opened one to get a better look but was halted by a squeal.

"It's not here!" shrieked Gassy, balancing on his good leg over the empty chest.

"What do you mean it's not there?" asked Borty.

"I mean it's not here. The freaking objective is empty."

"It's alright. They didn't say it would be in the chest. It must be here somewhere. Look ar—"

"Guys! Day Lord is coming," hummed Turdlet.

Confused by the sudden interruption, Gassy protested, "Don't be ridiculous. He wouldn't just show up out of the blue. We'd have some warning that he had arrived."

"Gassy's right. You're mistaken Turdlet, what are the guards doing?"

"No, but he really is coming. It's definitely him. All the guards have scarpered and everything. I promise, he's actually on his way."

"I told you, I couldn't give a doo doo what you think you see, tell us when he—"

"He's here," Turdlet yipped as he launched himself out the open window without looking, completely stunning the others.

"Huh?" Borty didn't have time to be shocked before the bedroom door slammed open.

On the other side was Day Lord.

He was a shiny man of such irradiating prowess that the lowly gnomes had to squint just to admire him. His skin seemed to catch the setting sun so completely that even his ornate helm paled in comparison. The density of Day Lord's muscles was so intense that they had their own gentle gravitational pull, or they would have but gravity hadn't been invented yet – so said many of his followers. In the presence of Day Lord's sparkly muscles, his armour clung so tightly to him that his piercing nipples could be seen glinting in the sunlight.

In awe of such a majestic being, Gassy and Borty were preparing themselves to beg for forgiveness and mercy. They never did that. Not once. And they were saved from begging this time too, as Day Lord looked at them. With a slow blink, he leaned forward. He continued to lean forward. In fact, he leant so far forward, and with such force, that his face cracked open on the stone floor of his own bedroom.

"Mr Day Lord, sir? Your tallness?" whimpered Gassy. On further inspection, Day Lord's sudden interest with the floor seemed to be caused by the long dagger sticking out the back of Day Lord's neck.

"Hmm," Borty hmmed at the scene unfolding before him, "I think he's dead...well... that was underwhelming."

Looking around, the gnomey pair noticed a shockingly gleeful boy standing right behind Day Lord's body.

It was Timmy.

"I killed him! My revenge is complete!" Timmy screamed with unbridled joy. His grin breaking the barriers of what could be considered a 'natural smile'.

"What, in the sweet..." Borty began before his thoughts trailed off.

"I'm going to live forever you stumpy fricks. Frick you and your dorky faces!" Timmy's insults continued in a rather reserved fashion given the murder he'd just commited. He then disappeared down the corridor, never to be seen by the gnomes again. Contrary to Timmy's belief, he did not live forever. In truth, he didn't even make it to the end of the day. Timmy's big head was splattered all over the pavement by a speeding elephoceros. Part elephant, part rhinoceros, and now a couple parts Timmy. Unfortunately for the young Timmy, he too had never learned one of life's most important lessons: road safety.

"I told you!" said Turdlet from outside the window. Much to his surprise, when jumping out the window he was comfortably caught by the stone floor of a very short balcony. "I bloody knew he would murder someone! At the top of page 41, didn't I say?"

"The book!" Gassy remembered, brushing past Turdlet's rather morbid, fourth-wall-breaking celebration.

"Right. It's probably on him. Check his pockets," suggested Borty.

"What pockets? He's wearing armour."

"Then take off his armour. Turdlet, get back in here and help us move the body." Turdlet immediately did as Borty suggested, shuffling his tuchus back in through the window. With a handful of careful heave-hos, the gnomes lugged the body into the room and locked the door behind them, as best they could. Piece-by-piece, they removed Day Lord's tight-fitting armour to see layer upon layer of rippling muscle.

"Now what?" asked Gassy, completely unaware that Borty was just making it up as he went along.

"I don't know. I honestly thought he'd be wearing something underneath. Somewhere to hide the Necrognomicon." To Borty's ever-expanding disappointment, Day Lord was absolutely stark naked under his armour. Were any of the gnomes of a particular persuasion, this might have been quite the exciting revelation (if we were to skirt past the small fact of Day Lord being one pulse short of alive).

"Where would he hide it? You saw how tight this stuff is. He couldn't have possibly hidden it anywhere that we wouldn't have already noticed by now. It's a hardback for gods' sake."

"I have an idea." Turdlet stepped in. The others waited patiently for his suggestion. His eyes slowly tracked Day Lord's body until they landed on something. Borty and

Gassy tracked his gaze line until they finally realised his glare was locked on Day Lord's glistening Daymoon.

"Don't be so stupid," started Borty, "he wouldn't. This is Day Lord we're talking about. An upper councilmember!"

"There's no way," added Gassy. Yet, contrary to their objections, Borty and Gassy didn't say another word as Turdlet lowered himself onto his hands and knees. He continued to deepen his stance. Lower. Lower. Until his chin was pressed against the cool stone floor as he gazed up into eternity.

"What do you see with your gnome eyes, Turdlet?" said Borty.

"There's something under there."

"No there fucking isn't," insisted Borty, midway between laughter and disbelief.

"What? Oh, no, not under Day Lord. All I can see under him is his perfectly pruned horizon. No, the bed." Turdlet pointed underneath Day Lord's magnificent bed. Without another word, Borty had slid the mattress off the four-poster to reveal a trapdoor.

"Help me with these slats," he demanded. One at a time, they carefully removed the bed slats, creating enough space to open the trapdoor. Borty wrapped his hand around the cast-iron handle and paused before pulling.

This is it, he thought.

With one swift tug, the trapdoor swung open. There it was. Inside the foot-deep hiding place, under a variable assortment of seemingly unimportant trinkets and knick-knacks, was the Necrognomicon.

"Lads. We've only gone and found it." It took everything in Borty's power to stop him from jumping up and down with joy.

"But we still need to get it to the hand-in point. Look at the size of that thing. We'll become an instant target to the other teams." Gassy's celebratory genes were more recessive than Borty's. He wasn't wrong though. The Necrognomicon was huge. Bound in gnome leather and pulling a rather silly face. At a glance, Gassy guessed it must have been well over two-thousand pages, each one likely filled with miraculous spells that could completely change the life of any honest gnome. It was beyond conspicuous.

Turdlet's less complicated thoughts went as follows: *I hope it has pictures.*

The cover seemed to crumble as they opened it. Not into pieces, but in the way dry mud might crumble off your boots. The silty layer fluttered through the air before disappearing into a shimmering dust. With a quick flick through, Turdlet's wildest thoughts came to life as they discovered page upon page of detailed illustrations.

"Flipping dora! Look at that enchantment! It really is the Necrognomicon." Gassy began to salivate at the book. *Think of what I could do with it*, he thought, *I could even finally make myself some loving friends.*

Gassy's depressingly lonely thoughts to one side, the gang was suddenly interrupted from their gawping by the sound of two hearty thumps on the door followed by a rather trepid voice.

"My all-lordiness, are you well?" the dainty voice began.

"Gassy, figure us a way out of here," demanded Borty as he passed the book to Turdlet. Gassy's immediate response was to awkwardly shrug his shoulders with very little in the way of plan of action after that.

"My all-lordiness? I do hope I'm not interrupting. I had heard a bit of a thump you see, but I would normally assume you were just tuckered out. Although, on this occasion, I did think it odd that a young boy would run past yelling 'I've killed Day Lord. I'm the person who killed Day Lord' and other such things. Silly, isn't it?" Taking advantage of the timorous fellow's one-sided conversation, Borty and Gassy scurried about the room trying to figure a way out that didn't involve execution.

"The balcony," suggested Gassy.

"I don't mean to be a bother, my all-lordiness, but the guards had also reported intruders having recently entered your bedroom. Not to mention the bodies lying in the corridor over there," the mysterious voice continued.

"That balcony's no good. Nowhere to go but back into the corridor. Too high up to get to the ground," said Turdlet.

"No tree or bush we could land in?"

"None from what I can tell. Just gravel." As Turdlet busied himself on the other side of the room, the pair stared out the window in hope of inspiration. Then it struck Gassy...

"We can go up!" he exclaimed.

"To the roof? That's further away from the ground. It's the ground we're trying to get to," mocked Borty.

"Yes. Thank you. But Breezy's MagInc portable ski-lift is on the roof." Gassy paused for praise. He found none.

"Right, we'll do that then," commanded Borty. When he turned back to Turdlet, he had the shock of his life. Turdlet, on the other hand, had never looked happier. There, encircling Turdlet, were three completely naked gnomes. Each one seemed dimmer than the last. Their bodies were covered in an oily mud that just barely kept their modesty.

"Where did they come from?" Gassy hesitantly questioned.

"The book."

"Elaborate," suggested Borty.

"This book."

"More elaboration is needed."

"There're quite a few gnome spells in this book. One of'em makes gnomes for a litt—"

Before Turdlet could finish his thought, their conversation was interrupted by an increasingly peeved peon rattling the door handle.

"Right! In just a little bit longer, I'm going to knock this door down. Any minute now," he cautiously warned.

"Roof time," demanded Borty.

"You two go, I'll keep them busy," Turdlet uncharacteristically offered. Sacrificing yourself so others could escape wasn't exactly the gnome way. It wasn't really anyone's way in this part of the world. And the few whose way it was rarely lasted long enough to see the sense in changing ways.

"Alright," Borty decided after very little consideration. The door thumping was getting louder now. "You distract them, we'll get away, then meet you at the rendezvous point if you survive."

"No," said Gassy.

"What do you mean 'no'?" Borty was almost as shocked as he was when finding the three extra gormless gnomes. Gassy, turning down a free sacrifice? And from Turdlet, no less? Madness.

"This isn't coming from a place of martyrdom. He's going to do something terrible to those gnomes."

"I'm not *going* to do something terrible to these gnomes." Turdlet innocently gasped.

"See. He's not going to do anything to those gnomes," affirmed Borty.

"What?! Did you not hear what he said? He clearly stressed 'going'. He said 'I'm not *going* to do something...' He's clearly already done something terrible."

"Turdlet, put Gassy's mind at ease. Have you or have you not done something awful to those gnomes?"

"No," assured Turdlet.

"See Gassy? He's clearly not done anything."

"You have to be flipping joking. What you asked him wasn't even a yes or no question! You're taking his side again. This is exactly like Coopgate." The room fell silent as Gassy said the C-word. Silent except for the increasingly distraught disciple behind door number one.

"How dare you say that word?" Borty was shocked. Appalled even. His opinion of Gassy had dropped even lower than his opinion of Turdlet.

"If the glove fits. This is exactly the same situation."

"It's not at all the same," insisted Borty.

"Yes, it is! He's done the same thing to those gnomes and it's going to scar us for life, just like Coopgate."

"Now you're just being dramatic," began Turdlet, "for starters there are significantly less chickens now than there were then."

"That's right! Not a chicken in sight, Gassy. Let's go to—"

"My all-lordiness!" an incredibly muscle-bound warrior whimpered as he plunged through the bedroom door. His soft, completely misfit voice left out a gentle moan as he spotted the fading corpse of his beloved lord, and in many ways, god. This majestic example of man's best is Sergeant Solomon Blacksteel. The very same enforcer the gnomes had witnessed separate people from their lower-halves, in the woods. His gentle demeanour hid what was possibly the worst day of his life. Not exclusively due to the loss of Day Lord either. Only a few minutes ago, the body of his younger brother was found outside the manor with a grappling-hook through his chest. Not moments after that, his only source of powdery comfort informed him of a sudden loss of supply, which he sorely needed after a long day's dismembering. This left Blacksteel's only remaining happiness dedicated to Day Lord.

All things considered, one could almost forgive him for picking up one of the muddied, nude gnomes by the leg and swinging it against the wall like he was trying to dust a carpet.

"To the roof then," suggested Gassy. Without a word, he and Borty snuck out the window and started to climb up to the roof, leaving Turdlet to fend for himself.

The slippery buttress that led them to the highest point in the manor was crumbling at the edges. Pieces that fell to the floor couldn't be heard shattering over the kafuffle coming from Day Lord's bedroom. With only a modicum of guilt, Gassy pulled his bloodied body up the sloped architectural feature thinking, *he'd definitely leave me if the roles were reversed.* Borty's thoughts were far more optimistic, reassuring himself that Turdlet always managed to get himself out of these kinds of situations.

The roof plateaued out. It was flat, with only the odd divot. Its edges were crenelated. Escape was just across from them, but between Borty and Gassy was an unwelcome obstacle.

"Breezy."

Chapter Fourteen

It was Breezy. Or it was at least ninety percent of him. Possibly even ninety-five. He was beside his ski-lift on the edge of the roof. Across his face were various tones of smeared blood mixed in with the gentle hint of personal puke. Even his teeth were splattered with blood. Blood that the gnomes suspected had something to do with his current hand situation. Hand seems like the appropriate descriptor, as the plural no longer applied to Breezy.

"Bloody hells!" exclaimed Borty, "he chewed his own hand off."

Borty's guess was spot on. Barely a few moments after being handcuffed and abandoned, Breezy decided that being found in Day Lord's keep would mean certain death. Even for him. So, he resorted to gently nibbling through his own arm. The task was laborious and incredibly painful which is why he gave up less than five minutes after breaking the skin on the back of his hand. That was also the moment he was beset by an overzealous guard. A few impressively powerful swings later, and Breezy was minus one hand. With his new freedom, he zapped the guard into pieces after grabbing a companion's essence-catalyst, and here we are.

"Gassy Bedchambers. I expected so much more from you." Breezy groaned as he failed to boost himself off a crenellation into the ski-lift.

"I know you're in pain, Breezy, but we don't have time for this. We all need to get off this roof before the guards find us," said Gassy.

"Hand over the book and I will let you on," smirked Breezy.

Looking at Borty, Gassy waited. Borty looked back with an equal amount of expectation. Their eyes darted back and forth to Breezy, both of them expecting the other to hand it over. They both knew they could overpower him once they were off the roof. After a few seconds of this silent back-and-forth, they figured it out.

"Turdlet has it," they announced in disappointed unison.

"Then we will be waiting for him." Breezy leant against the ski-lift with one hand on his waist and the other in a bloodied bag on his side.

"If we wait, we'll be caught!" Borty's patience with this pest was wearing thin.

"*You* will be caught. I would not dare be arrested by some lowly meat-for-brains militia." Even his weak insults sounded plagiarised.

"The light strollers are back, Breezy," said Gassy. "Day Lord and his enforcer are back." Breezy paused for a moment. Another error in his plan? Impossible.

"Nobody is going anywhere," Breezy stepped forward and brandished his missing stump at Gassy and Borty, "until we use the book to correct this little mistake."

An unusual phenomenon will often happen to those that recently attempt to chew off their own hand. This very specific problem comes when losing one's sense of one's self.

From the day you are born, second by second you are learning about yourself. Part of this journey of self-discovery comes in the form of learning the limits of your body, quite literally. Without thinking about it, every day you are unconsciously paying careful attention to the ends of your fingertips, the length of your arms, the breadth of your chest. These self-evaluations tally up, little by little, and create an internal schematic in your subconscious, one that's even more unchanging for a gnome who starts life as an adult. But when the outside suddenly doesn't quite match your body's schematic, basic activities like trying to wipe your own arse can end in embarrassment.

Once Breezy had finished wagging his phantom fingers at Borty and Gassy, he reached out to his ski-lift to lean on it once more. That was his first mistake. After not quite accounting for the sudden disappearance of six inches of his arm, Breezy slipped. Not the end of the world, you might think. He can recover from that. Well, the fright of missing his grip at such a precarious position flicked his reflexes on which flung his arm back towards the ski-lift only to fall short for the second time. Slipping off the edge of the tallest building in town was enough reason to spark a flailing fear in Breezy. He flung both his arms towards the ski-lift as if they could anchor him to the rooftop, only to be sourly disappointed by both his hands missing the grapple-point. He was too far. He was going to fall.

From where Borty and Gassy stood, they saw a slightly less comprehensible turn of events. They watched Breezy battle with himself over the course of less than a couple of seconds, only to disappear off the edge, but not without getting the last word in, "Bugger."

Their surprise was quickly interrupted by the sound of screaming and an alarm bell. They rushed to the edge of the reinforced manor's parapet to see all the yard guards were headed in their direction. Directly below the pair was a mangled version of Breezy, barely in two pieces.

"Is he still moving?" Gassy queried, squinting his eyes.

"Doesn't matter. It's time to go," commanded Borty.

"There's still a little time. We can wait for Turdlet."

"We don't need to."

"But he has the book."

145

"Gassy, don't worry. He's not the type to self-sacrifice. He'll figure something out and we'll see again him soon." Borty hopped into the portable ski-lift and turned on the motor. He turned to Gassy and reached out his hand.

"That's part of my worries," said Gassy, taking Borty's hand. "He tends to get creative in a pickle and I don't like that."

Once they were both settled, the ski-lift began. Pistons and pipes, levers and gears, they all spurred into motion when their floating cabin sputtered towards the next rooftop. Neither of them had ever seen such remarkable technology and wouldn't have had a clue how to operate it if it weren't for the delightfully convenient illustrations on the side of the motor. Together they cranked and winded various parts until they reached the maximum speed of three miles per hour.

In their leisurely cruise to escape, no guard had noticed them. They were scot-free. Well, unless you include Turdlet. The pair sat at the back of the cabin, looking back at the manor house with a shared concern.

"I'm sure he'll be fine," insisted Borty. More and more guards flooded into the manor yelling things like 'kill the intruders' and 'death to thieves'.

"We really should have taken the Necrognomicon with us." Gassy glared at the manor. "Oh gods! I hope Josi is okay."

"Who?"

"You know. That lovely chef with the delicious trifles."

"Oh. I'm sure she's fine. When have you ever known a guard to persecute the wrong person?" Borty stifled a laugh as Gassy looked more worried for Josi than he ever was for Turdlet.

Completely without warning, the entire manor went up in flames as a series of explosions fractured every wall. Breath-to-breath, windows and warriors were shattered by the sounds of a dozen separate explosions all resonating from inside Day Lord's manor. Gassy and Borty weren't even surprised. If anything, they were surprised by their lack of surprise. Unsurprisingly, they knew the culprit. They didn't know how he did it, but Turdlet was behind this.

"If he survives this one, we're going to have words." Borty wasn't even mad, just disappointed. He wasn't against the reckless destruction of other people's property, but he certainly preferred to know if it was going to happen, especially if he was – until recently – on the top of said property.

The smell of smoke and charred meat suddenly permeated the air.

Snap. The cabin jolted. It felt as if it dropped a little.

"What was that?" asked Gassy. He preferred not to guess, but it was clear it wasn't going to be someone playing an enthusiastic game of cards.

Snap. The noise went again. It continued, with increased frequency. If it *were* a game of cards, someone was doing very well.

Gassy popped his head out the window to inspect the noise. There, where the cabin met the chain it travelled across, was a 'jam' in the mechanism – 'jam' being the more courteous description but a more accurate one would be a 'dismembered limb'. The incredible mechanical power of this ski-lift wasn't halted by some simpleton's arm. It was stopped by the sword the hand carried. As the gears struggled to crumple through the foreign object, the sword strained the cabin's connector until some of its bolts began to *snap*.

"We're going to fall," Gassy calmly stated as he climbed back into the cabin. Explosions continued behind them.

"Really? Why does this always happen?"

"You mean the explosions!? Because you keep trusting Turdlet! We could have gone with anyone else but you chose him again."

"No, not the explosions. I mean, whenever we're balancing precariously over a potentially lethal fall, whatever we're on always seems to break."

Thinking back on it, Gassy couldn't think of a single example to prove Borty wrong. And it wasn't like this was a rare occurrence. They were beginning to make a habit of it. They must have been in a situation almost exactly like this in their previous six heists before Gassy took time off.

"Huh," he said, "I guess you're right. The usual position then?"

"How's it breaking?" Borty asked as the cabin groaned.

"From the connector."

"Ah, the usual then. Sit that botty down," commanded Borty. Hardly a second passed after they sat back in their seats before the cabin completely detached from its chain. It fell. A perfectly straight fall. The sinking metal box picked up speed. Gassy grabbed Borty's hand as he tensed up. Borty smiled as they fell. Just as the world was drowned out by the sound of wind rushing by their ears, it suddenly crashed back into existence.

"Ahhh! My coccyx!" yelled Gassy. His pained gasp could barely be heard over the screams from outside their cabin.

"Now's not the time to be thinking about your little codger." Borty pulled himself from his seat and shuffled out of the half-crumpled cabin. What met him was chaos. Every kind of race was scattering from the scene of the explosion in varying levels of panic. Parents carried their children, farmers carried their livestock, carpenters carried their furniture – or at least he assumed that was the scenario and it wasn't just people making off with whatever they felt like. Deadly debris shattered the spirits of the town's citizens. Pieces of rogue rock blew holes in the sides of buildings as they were peppered with gravel and hot glass.

Just ahead, Gassy and Borty noticed fluttering embers swirling to the floor. The sizzling embers burned different colours. Blues, reds, yellows, purples, and other familiar colours. It was beautiful, but it signified a loss far greater than any life.

"The ribbons!" exclaimed Gassy. The river of ribbon that ran through the streets was ablaze and spreading fast.

"Quick, find the black and green ribbon."

As fast as their little legs could take them, they sprinted under the fiery clouds doing their best to catch a glimpse of the escaping black ribbon. Gassy's leg gash slowed them down, and had started to pulsate with serious pain, but they managed to just about stay ahead of the flames. After a few streets, they discovered it. The black ribbon ran up a small, forested hilltop, the opposite direction the crowds were running in. They all seemed to be heading for the port.

"Which way?" asked Gassy, gesturing to the panicked people. They seemed to know what to do. Abandoning the mission wasn't an option. But they didn't have the Necrognomicon. Turdlet did. What would Turdlet do?

"We go up the hill. Turdlet is waiting for us."

It was thirty minutes after Borty and Gassy reached the hilltop. The black ribbon – which they had to extinguish before it set the trees on fire – ran all the way to a submerged hovel. The tattered door had a crudely drawn sign on it that said 'Cungratsulashons'. Seemed like the right place, especially since it was mostly underground.

The gnomes had seen the odd person enter since they'd been waiting, but they didn't dare enter themselves. They were waiting for Turdlet.

Gassy sat on a mushroom-foam toadstool, looking back out towards the town. There, in his squishy little chair, he watched Under-arraz (sigh) perish. It was a surprise it hadn't happened sooner really. *How didn't it happen last time there was a fire?* Gassy thought to himself.

"Pretty crazy, huh?" Borty was rarely unsure what to say, but right now was one of those moments.

"Crazy. What a health and safety hazard. Why did anyone think those ribbons were a good idea?"

"Exactly! They should have expected a rogue explosion in the middle of the town. This kind of thing happens all the time."

"*All* the time." Gassy frowned with an agreeing disbelief.

"Still, it's very pretty."

"Oh, *so* pretty. Lovely colours. Even the fires are multi-coloured. And the enchantments are still active, so there's hardly any smoke." Just as Gassy mentioned the enchantments, the town's chirpy bright fire suddenly switched to a swirling vortex of black smoke clouds blotting out the light, as if to match the mood of their next conversation.

"Oop, there they go. Well not every enchantment is built to last...so...Turdlet," Borty soberly began, "he should be here by now."

Gassy grasped his hands and shuffled in his fungus, "He's still got time."

"Yeah, you're right. He could just be running late." Borty was hesitant with each word.

"He's an idiot. He probably just got lost," Gassy's face creased enough to just about resemble a smile.

"I'm sure that's what's hap—"

"He's probably even handed it in already," Gassy nervously giggled. "Knowing him, he's already taken the reward and started stirring up trouble somewhere else."

Borty paused for a moment before speaking, "Maybe. But we do have eyes on the end goal. If someone hands in the book, we'll know." Borty's soft tone wasn't doing much to sooth Gassy.

"Then he's taken the book for himself. You know how he is, if he enjoys something you know he'll take it too far," reasoned Gassy.

The occasional criminal crept up the hill, empty-handed and disappointed. Each one that seemed a little short stopped the conversation. Even someone far away managed to delay the odd syllable as the gnomes discovered the deception of depth perception. There grew an undeniable fact that they couldn't forget. The inferno was spiralling out of control. Anyone left in there would soon be dead. Very soon. Only those resistant to fire would bother continuing the search for the Necrognomicon, and even those few individuals erred on the side of caution since their protection against fire doesn't protect against a collapsing building – which funnily enough would be the same phrase uttered to thousands of under-arrazites as they made their home insurance claims over the coming weeks.

No, in a tinderbox town like that, there was no way anyone was coming back in one piece. Not if they were at the fire's very epicentre. No way. It would be nothing short of magic.

At the edge of defeat, Borty and Gassy took one last look at the burning town together.

"We failed then. Again. There's a reason I didn't want to leave my home, you know," said Gassy.

"Yeah. We can't win without Turdlet," sighed Borty. "But failure isn't all that bad. At least we both got out alive."

Gassy smiled at Borty. Maybe he was right.

It wasn't all bad.

In the joyful crackle of the burning town, the gnomes could hear something. A soft whistle. This whistle got louder and louder but remained the same kind of pitch.

"Where's that coming from?" Gassy asked when he noticed Borty looking into the sky.

"That's unexpected," said Borty. Before Gassy could see what Borty saw, the whistling was suddenly replaced by the thundering crash of tumbling timber and rustling leaves.

"What in the gods!?" They hurried over to the sound that had already garnered the attention of a few other nearby criminals.

It was Turdlet. He was clasping the book in both his hands. His sturdy botty was generously embedded halfway up an elder oak tree.

"I'm alright!" he yelled. His hood and hair were in such a state that a less observant gnome wouldn't have noticed his eyes were on the verge of popping out of his head. Even more alarming was how they slunk back into their sockets after a painfully slow and robotic blink.

"You're alive!" cried Gassy, "we both thought you were blown to pieces, or burned, or stabbed by the guards, or crushed under buildings, or trampled by crowds, or ambushed by other thieves..." Gassy's listing continued as Borty managed to free Turdlet from the tree.

"Care to explain why you're arse-first in a tree?" asked Borty.

"A spell. This book has a ton of weird spells. All of them gnome related." Turdlet brushed himself off, holding the Necrognomicon to his chest. "Turns out, flying ain't easy fellas."

Gassy stopped listing as he inspected the shimmering book. "And how did you find us?"

"Yeah. Like I said, all sorts of spells. Look." Turdlet gave an example by healing the gash in Gassy's leg in almost an instant. All of their eyes widened.

"I don't suppose one of those spells is the reason that the manor house exploded?" asked Borty.

"No."

Looking at each other, both Borty and Gassy silently agreed that Turdlet was full of shit.

"I ruddy knew it! He said he wouldn't blow anything up, right from the start, and was lying. He *did* do something to those gnomes." Gassy was absolutely livid. Inconsolable, even. "This is *exactly* like Coopgate. Even if there are fewer chickens, he did the same bloody thing."

"Woah! I resent that remark," began Turdlet, "I didn't put *any* explosives inside those gnomes. They were summoned with explosive mud around them. I just told them where to blow up."

"Boys. Now's not the—"

"You 'just told them where to *blow up*'?! Are you pretending like creating life just to make an explosion is normal?" Gassy's lividity only escalated.

"Fellas. Best keep it down—"

"I only did what I had to. If I hadn't, you'd both be dead. Took everything I had, and the book had, just to keep that big chunky guard from crushing me into a pasty mess."

"Oi! Gnomes!" yelled Borty. He gestured around them. Hidden behind trees, glancing from their seats in the grass, or just blatantly staring at them, criminals of every miniature kind were listening into their heated conversation. Once their attention was brought to the audience, Gassy and Turdlet immediately shut up. They knew they'd made a mistake.

"We hand it in. This thing is too dangerous for us to keep," insisted Borty. Much to Turdlet's disappointment, he still agreed almost as quickly as Gassy. Without serious power to back it up, carrying a spellbook like that around was like wearing a sign saying: 'Please Murder Me.'

"Fine. But I'm keeping the next cool thing we steal."

Chapter Fifteen

Knock Knock. The gnomes stood under a subsurface veranda. On the tattered 'Cungratsulashons' door were scratches and signs of weathering from decades ago. The mound this hovel was built into was clearly older than it looked at first glance.

"It's open," one rather grumpy sounding voice called from beyond the door. Looking around, the gnomes noticed every criminal that was previously milling about was now watching their moves carefully. Only one option then. Borty took the lead. He grabbed the handle and, with the confidence of a gnome who knew what he was doing, he marched through the door.

Inside was what can only be structurally described as a one-scoop ice-cream cone. The gnomes walked into a roughly dome-shaped room to see criminals waiting along its edges. In the middle of the room was a ladder stretching over a deep fall into a honeycomb like housing space. Little beds sparsely populated the occasional alcove, each with their own personal two-way ladder, or staircase, crossing in and over the cone structure.

Immediately ahead, across the cetral ladder, was a door. A door that said 'Hand in' above it, in perfect cursive. There was plenty of space along the dome wall to skirt the edges and reach the door, but everywhere they looked, a new criminal emerged with a hunger in their eyes.

"I don't suppose you planned for this, Gassy?" Borty was reaching around his person, carefully readying himself for a fight.

"No. How could I? Whatever is happening here is not normal."

"Gassy, in case we die today, I need you to know something." Turdlet stared at his tubby compatriot gathering every ounce of his attention.

"Yeah? Shoot."

"Gassy. You are... a big baby boy."

"Oh for fu—"

"It is the Necrognomicon! Everyone, see here!" One of the criminals called out. A fae, no less. Typical.

"We should have expected this," said Borty as dozing crime-doers awakened. "Of course they wouldn't play by the rules. Turdlet, anything you can do right now would be useful."

Turdlet rested the Necrognomicon on his arm and was opening it before a threatening voice bellowed from their encirclement.

"You crack the spine on that book, little gnome, and I'll crack yours." Coupled with the voice came the sound of blades being slowly drawn from their sheaths. There were so many people, it was hard to tell who even said it. Turdlet halted.

"Do you know any spells from memory?" whispered Borty.

"The book doesn't work unless I open it," said Turdlet.

The gnomes froze. They didn't know what to do.

Gassy quickly whipped his head around checking for signs of exits. He saw none. However, he did notice his competitors flinch with almost every movement he made. Most already had their various weapons drawn, but concealed.

"I have an idea," said Gassy.

The others didn't know how to respond. *Gassy is never spontaneous*, they thought. They were convinced he wouldn't try something new without overthinking it in a dozen different ways.

"Give me the book," he said.

He gestured to Turdlet who was slowly pulling the crossbow from his back. Unsure what to do, he looked to Borty who agreed that he should pass the Necrognomicon over.

"It better be a good idea," said Turdlet while handing over the book.

With book in hand, everyone around the room watched Gassy. They salivated like a pack of wolves waiting for the cat hanging-in-there to fall.

"You're all cowards!" declared Gassy, to the shock of his companions. "None of you have what it takes to be this year's winner."

"Uh, Gassy? Not the best play," said Borty.

Gassy continued. "Oh yes. Not one of you here came even close to taking this book, otherwise you'd be dead. You're all a bunch of wimps."

"I'm with Borty here. What're you doing?" Turdlet raised his little crossbow as he noticed the looming criminals.

"That's right. You're all soft and weak. I don't reckon a single one of you could take this book if you tried, so we'll give you a chance. Here, fight for it." As Gassy taunted his captivated audience, he threw the Necrognomicon into the bottom of the cone-shaped pit. It fell almost five gnomes in height before settling on a ladder crossing.

Other gnomes, fae, fairies, troglites, demi-ogres, gobbas, oakmites, dyaws, and one particularly short human all failed to move. The first one in would certainly be killed.

"All of you back-off" yelled the only human who definitely wasn't insecure about his height, "I'm the tallest and therefore the best. I deserve it."

"We'll rip out your gigantic eyes, you freak," yelled a small swarm of fairies in unison, as if they had practiced the threat but only a couple times so hadn't quite nailed the execution. "The book is ours."

"No, I," said the troglite, he wasn't even sure what they were arguing over.

"No, me's."

"No, ours."

"No, nobody's. We should burn it," suggested one unpopular fresh-faced gnome who was imminently crushed under the weight of the demi-ogre's war hammer.

"Agreed. That was a stupid suggestion," announced a recognisable voice. It was a microtroll.

Slinking into the quietest spot in the room, Gassy murmured to himself "Turkey?"

It was indeed Turkey. She was strangely well-equipped. Leagues ahead, actually. Beside her, dressed from head-to-toe in spikey plated armour, was her ID.

"So, how are we going to settle this, fellas?"

"You should fight!" yelled Turdlet. All three of our heroic gnomes were now hiding behind a turned-over table.

"Yeah, fight!" added Gassy.

"Kill them all, Turkey." Borty was ready to start taking bets.

Their calls were enough to tip everyone over the edge. There were an easy fifty people in this ice-cream cone and all of them instantly tried to backstab, cut-throat, snipe, or stealthily eliminate the nearest person. The demi-ogre would have tried to pop someone else if he wasn't one of the first deaths.

In seconds, the population of the room halved.

"Wow. I guess that's what happens if you have a room full of assassins and thieves." Gassy's commentary was overshadowed by Borty and Turdlet taking bets.

"4-to-1 on the microtroll? Are you mad? She's big, sure, but she's the main target. Everyone will want a piece. It's literally five against one right now!" raged Borty.

"Listen buddy, I don't make the odds. That's just how they are," Turdlet continued after he watched Turkey decapitate another victim as she retreated onto the central ladder, "make that 2-to-1."

"C'mon!" he yelled, deliberating the bet, "...fine, a hundred pieces on Turkey and her ID."

Bets taken. Seats found. Twenty-five left standing. Eleven teams remain. One fairy swarm left. The gnomes settled in for a show.

The violence accelerated with the gobbas, as most fights did. They dashed around the room. Each dash added a new cut to their foes and started a new fight between teams.

The fae released a chaotic spell. It spiralled nowhere good, vaporised most of the fairies and eviscerated a ladder holding up some chunky troglites. They tumbled all the way down and settled right beside the Necrognomicon. Their close proximity caused all fighting to leap into the pit. Unfortunately for Gassy, there were a few strays with keen eyes.

"Die!" an aggressive gnome screamed as he lunged at Gassy with a serrated blade. That attacker was stopped in his tracks when a small crossbow bolt penetrated through the bottom of his chin, killing him instantly.

"Lords above!" shrieked Gassy as he looked to his saviour. Beside him, Turdlet was reloading his little crossbow.

"I don't think we can sit this one out, boys," declared Borty. "Turdlet, make sure the book ends up in our hands. I'll take care of Gassy." With a nod of confirmation, Turdlet leapt over the table and dived straight into the pit below.

On his way down, Turdlet drew his dagger and plunged it into a troglite to slow his descent down.

Just a few steps down, Oakmites held sturdy with the book in their hands. They blocked blades with their bark. They fought back with their trunks. A kick. A punch. Two dead dyaws. Two more dyaws, out for revenge, took long meaningful swings with their wetted axes, timbering the oakmites with a crunching confidence.

A rouge mace shattered the air in front of Turdlet. Falling short, Turdlet had time to draw his crossbow with his other hand. His aggressor was the last troglite.

It swung again. Another miss.

He fired his bolt, a grazing blow.

A jab pushed Turdlet on his back. He launched his blade but it didn't connect. Turdlet parried another swing. It was heavy. The kind of heavy that would kill instantly. One more strike approached but was halted by two girthy arms wrapping around the troglite's throat. It was Turkey.

Turdlet shuffled back, noticing a dyaw trying to make off with the Necrognomicon. It scurried up the nearest ladder with the book just to be sniped down by Turdlet's crossbow.

Back in the scoop area, Borty and Gassy weren't struggling to fend off the stragglers. Their attempts were weak and without any serious coordination. These 'criminals' seemed more like the team servants which didn't really make Gassy feel much better about himself. Their rather dull squabbling was uneventful enough for Gassy to notice a nearby figure rummaging in the walls.

"I bloody knew it!" Gassy declared as Borty quickly dispatched the remaining glorified team-backpacks.

"What is it?" asked Borty.

Gassy responded by pointing.

It was Breezy.

"Great," said Borty. "I'm going to feel bad beating up a one-armed gnome."

As if he tested fate, Borty watched as Breezy pulled something out of the wall. He instantly recognised it. It was a bottle, with a shimmering pink liquid inside. Breezy downed it in seconds.

"That's not what I think it is, right?" Gassy asked.

"I think it is," said Borty.

The pair watched, helpless, as Breezy's missing arm was given a fresh replacement. He dropped the luxurious empty bottle and turned to the gnomes, 'essence catalyst' in hand.

"Rush him," commanded Borty. Borty sprinted towards Breezy as Gassy hesitated. With a flash and a crackle, Borty was singed from top to bottom. He keeled over mid-sprint, unable to move as his relatively handsome appearance melted away into a distant memory.

"That felt remarkable!" declared Breezy. "What a relief. I knew my plans would finally outplay you all. This is why being so well-prepared is important."

Gassy rushed over to Borty with tears teetering on his eye lids. Borty was still breathing, with his eyes wide open, but he couldn't focus them on Gassy.

"Do not be sad, Gassy. Soon you will realise I have done you a favour. They do not deserve to have you in their team. You are free," said Breezy.

"He's going to die," said Gassy.

"Let him. With a good plan, you won't need him anymore."

At that same moment Turdlet emerged from the cone pit with the Necrognomicon in hand. His eyes locked onto Gassy who was hunched over Borty.

"Borty!?" he bellowed, oblivious to the attention he'd garnered from Breezy.

"The book," yelled Breezy. "Give it to me, you mistake."

Turdlet watched Gassy's tears running down his face. He was presented a choice. Turdlet had nothing to gain from helping Gassy, and everything to gain from just leaving. Everything being, his life. And yet, Turdlet hesitated.

"The thing is, Breezy, you're a bit of a twat. So, I think I'll keep the book." In that moment, Turdlet charged Breezy, using the book as his shield and loosing a crossbow bolt. At the same time, Breezy released a burst of essence towards Turdlet. The essence crashed into the Necrognomicon, creating a shockwave of power that launched Turdlet back into the pit. Breezy, unable to hold his footing, was disarmed and thrown to the ground, narrowly avoiding Turdlet's crossbow bolt.

On the floor, Breezy panicked as he realised his weapon was nowhere to be seen, until he noticed something. The Necrognomicon was lying right beside him.

With Turdlet out of the picture, Breezy rose to his feet with a smile on his face and the Necrognomicon in his hands.

"Gassy, my boy, it is time I show you what real magi...essence is." Breezy pressed his hand against the Necrognomicon. He whispered the words of the book. Dark swirls of 'essence' started to encage him. Suddenly, a sharp beam of green essence zigged through Breezy, cutting his body from top to bottom. The dark 'essence' stopped instantly.

"Was this part of your plan?" Gassy was holding Breezy's magic wand. Breezy frowned. He tried to talk but, without warning, his body collapsed into an unorganised mess of parts.

Gassy paused for a moment. He could hear Borty spluttering beside him, struggling to catch his breath and choking on any breath he caught, yet Gassy couldn't look away from the mess that was Breezy.

A mostly unscathed Turdlet emerged from the pit again, and immediately rushed over to Gassy who was now hovered over Borty's fading body.

"We need to get him some help. Grab his legs," said Turdlet.

"Help from the town we just burnt down?" said Gassy. Turdlet squatted over Borty's legs. He knew Gassy was right. Then suddenly, it clicked.

"The Necrognomicon!" he sprinted over to the scorched book, now soaked with the gooier parts of Breezy. He opened the book to a spell he thought might work. His smile dropped.

"Quickly!" said Gassy. Turdlet didn't hurry. "What's the matter?"

"I can't do this," said Turdlet. "He's too far gone. It's too difficult. I'd end up killing him."

"Well we need to at least try!" Gassy's tears streamed down his face. Turdlet hung his head. He didn't dare look at Gassy as he pushed the Necrognomicon into his hands.

"You do it."

"What do you mean? If you can't do it, there's no way I can," whimpered Gassy.

"Gassy, let's be serious. You're the only one that can do this," said Turdlet.

"What?"

"Look. You're better at this than me. I'm worlds better at thieving and fighting and most other things, obviously, but there is something you know better than me. That something is magic. You are the only one that can do this. The only one that can save Borty." Turdlet pushed the Necrognomicon deeper into Gassy's hands.

Completely shocked, Gassy did as he was told. He scanned the pages of the book. Illustrations, symbols, and words all joined together. From him birthed dark swirls of magic that orbited his crouched position. They spun around him, gaining speed and brushing air across his chubby cheeks. The smell of iron pilfered his sense of smell.

"I need a donation for his body!" yelled Gassy as the magic roared with a vibrating energy. Turdlet shrugged his shoulders, not understanding what Gassy needed. Gassy then spotted the mess that was their rival. He reached out his hand and the magic formed in front of him. It scooped up parts of Breezy's body and launched them into Borty. In a burst, Borty was thrown to his feet.

"Lords above!" he screamed as he patted down his body. The gnomes embraced him without hesitation. "I'm not dead!"

"You're not dead!" confirmed Gassy.

"This feels very odd." Borty squished the fleshy parts of his face that were very recently erring on the crispier side of toast.

"Are you okay?" asked Gassy.

"Yeah...I think so."

"We might not be for much longer." Turdlet gestured to the ongoing battle that was slowly seeping out of the conelike pit.

"Let's hand this book in," said Borty. "Move!"

Chapter Sixteen

"Gentlemen, congratulations," a dapperly dressed dwaff declared. A dwaff – much like every other race, species, location, or invention mentioned thus far – is a completely original being with absolutely no qualities taken from anything outside the public domain. That being said, this sturdy-looking dwaff was about as short as the gnomes but built like a brick house. He was incredibly well-groomed and clearly took pride in his appearance which would be understandable when you look that good. With every word he pleasantly hummed there was an air of unfuckwithability.

His room was a far cry from the battleground the gnomes left behind them. It was small, not much bigger than a broom cupboard, with wooden carvings all around. On closer inspection, Gassy noticed that the table was carved from wood but was also fused with the wall. It didn't take long for him to realise they were standing inside a rather girthy repurposed tree trunk, now decorated with such a grand level of gaudiness that would make even a fae shake with envy.

"We win then?" asked Borty as he wiped his bloodied hands on his clothes. There was a banging on the door that everyone ignored.

"Yes. You win. But before we get to business, I'll have to ask you gentlemen to clean yourselves before you can sit down." The dwaff finished his thought as Turdlet was inches away from settling his botty. "There's a fountain over there."

The fountain the dwaff pointed to looked suspiciously like a bidet. Once they were all spotless, they found their way to their seats. The door rattled again with a heavier banging.

"Is that a companion of yours?" queried the dwaff.

"Nah, we're all here," announced Turdlet.

"Curious. Everyone knows the rules. You've made it in and clearly have the target. The competition is over."

The room fell silent for the moment as they heard yelling, screaming, and the clash of more blades. Borty broke the quiet, "Some people are just persistent I suppose."

"No matter. Persistence will get them nowhere, and certainly not through that door," the dwaff began. "My name is Mr Lawderman. I'll be certifying the authenticity of your acquisition today."

Mr Lawderman got to his feet and shook each of the gnome's freshly cleaned hands.

"You don't need to be so formal. We would rather things be done quickly," said Borty.

"Demeanour decides the dwaff, Mr Beetle-bowel," All the gnomes were shocked to hear Borty's name. "Now, would you be so kind as to hand me the Necrognomicon."

"Wait. How do you know my name?"

"You filled out a waiver," said Mr Lawderman, brandishing three signed forms from the competition entry.

"He's right. We did do that," announced Gassy.

"Yes. Thank you Gassy." Borty looked at Turdlet who was now hugging the Necrognomicon and telegraphed all he needed to know with a simple calm nod. Reluctantly, Turdlet released his grip on the book.

Mr Lawderman carefully donned some leather gloves before taking the book. He dropped his glasses onto the bridge of his nose, the kind with an unknown exotic animal strap wrapping around the back of his head. He shortened his breath as he inspected the cover.

"This isn't its original condition," said the dwaff, noting the web like burns on the front.

"There were a few complications. But nothing we couldn't handle," said Borty. He smiled.

"And you couldn't avoid this kind of damage?"

"Some damage was unavoidable. But all the pages should be intact," said Borty with a shrug.

"At the risk of sounding ridiculously obtuse, why?"

The gnomes didn't quite know how to respond to his question, looking to each other for answers only to find equally confused faces.

"Why what, sir?" asked Gassy.

"Why was damage unavoidable?" Mr Lawderman's tone was like a teacher scolding their student. Like he'd just found them eating glue and was trying to get them to understand why that was a bad thing to do.

"Erm..." Gassy began as confidently as he continued, "we were in a lot of danger. In some cases, it was the book or us."

"And you chose yourselves." Mr Lawderman phrased his statement like a statement, yet he paused for a moment as if waiting for a response to a question. As Gassy was about to try to answer his non-question, Mr Lawderman returned to his inspection of the book. He flicked through page after page, only looking up to scorn anyone who dared to so much as clear their throat. After inspecting more than half the book, he stopped and slammed it wide open.

"Where are these pages?"

"What pages?" asked Borty, genuinely unsure what was happening now.

Mr Lawderman held the Necrognomicon in his hands and leant it forward showing the gnomes that six pages had been carelessly torn from the book; a whole section. They were situated right before the *Life After Death* section.

"Are you going to tell me you had nothing to do with this?" asked Mr Lawderman.

"We honestly have no idea where those pages are. It must have been like that when we got it," said Borty.

"We hardly had a chance to even look at it before our escape began," argued Gassy.

Turdlet was suspiciously quiet. His silence didn't go unnoticed.

"And you?" said Mr Lawderman, his accusatory tone directed at Turdlet, "Do you know where these pages are?"

"Nope." Everyone expected him to expand on his response just a little bit, but he seemed so sure of himself. Not a hint of nervousness or fear seeped out of him. He just stared.

Mr Lawderman was certain nobody would be stupid enough to try to steal from him while lying about it with such confidence. He settled back in his seat.

"Most of it seems to be here. It's a shame about those other spells, potent as they were, but MagInc will be able to take care of these ones."

"Wait," said Borty, putting his hand on the carved table, "MagInc?"

"That's right. They're this year's sponsor. Didn't you know?" said Mr Lawderman.

"You mean for Breezy's team, right?"

"No. Not just that useless team. The whole competition. In fact, they sponsored the entirety of Crimicon this year."

It wasn't that much of a surprise. They had money everywhere, so why not sponsor Crimicon? They *were* the king of criminals, after all. MagInc somehow made a killing skirting or moving the line of the law to get away with acts that would be considered barbaric tyranny were there no money involved. Yet, this particular sponsor put Borty in a place of unease the others couldn't understand.

"The Necrognomicon is going to them?" asked Turdlet.

Closing up the book, mostly satisfied, Mr Lawderman said, "That's right. No one man should have the power this book has, it's best put in the hands of an organisation who already has power. You can't abuse power when you already have so much experience managing it."

He took to his feet, grabbed his coat and a rather fashionable satchel. Book stored away in his bag, he turned back to the gnomes.

"Ah, yes. Your reward." They'd almost completely forgotten their payment, and would have likely let Mr Lawderman leave if he hadn't mentioned it himself.

Quickly overcoming his discomfort, Borty leaned forward in his chair with eagerness. Mr Lawderman slid one of the desk's draws open and produced a gold-trimmed box from inside.

"Oh, and, MagInc holds no responsibility for any harm you may deal or receive in use of the contents of this box." He placed it purposefully with a there-you-go attitude and disappeared outside through a hidden door at the back of the tree trunk, without the gnomes noticing.

Their eyes fixed on the box. The gnomes congratulated themselves.

"We did it, boys," said Borty.

* * * * *

She hadn't had a battle like that in months. Years even. She'd forgotten how good it felt to out-perform people who made killing their profession. But this time was different. It was the most challenging fight she'd ever had. She had to admit that if some of her opponents had been at full fighting strength when she faced them, she would be dead. Still, it didn't take much away from how good it felt to stand on the ladder balancing over the pit, lording over the bodies of lesser criminals.

As her bloodlust softened, and the feeling rushed back into her limbs with a resounding vengeance, Turkey noticed the gnomes leaving their meeting. They weren't in the celebratory mood she expected.

"You gnomes started this mess and left me to finish it!" she brandished her stolen war axe thinking there was no harm in adding a few more delinquents to her body count, as soon as she could make her way over to them, one careful step at a time.

"You didn't have to fight them," said Borty.

"Yes, I did. If I stopped, I would be dead."

"Then just leave? They wouldn't have bothered to stop you," said Gassy.

"What a wonderful idea, why didn't I think of that?" said Turkey drenched in sarcasm, "oh wait, because both the doors were locked!"

Looking at each other, the gnomes apathetically shrugged.

"You can't blame us for that," said Turdlet, "we didn't lock the doors."

"Oh, I *can* blame you for that and I will." Turkey threw her axe at the gnomes, comfortably missing them. "It's your reckless, destructive approach to the competition that caused this. But I might just let you go if you hand over the reward."

Borty looked at her, then at the reward, then at the gnomes. None of them expressed a slither of surprise, nor any other emotion really. Nothing more complex that subtle sleepiness.

"You can have the reward," said Turdlet, throwing her the box.

Turkey dropped her backup axe to catch the box, hardly believing her luck. She hurriedly opened it before the gnomes changed their mind. Inside she saw two pieces of paper and a little bag.

"Twenty percent off your next MagInc purchase, a three-week warranty for the box, and..." she rustled into the little bag, "a cut-throat shaving kit."

The gnomes nodded, knowing full well they'd already taken the cash prize out the box which just about covered expenses. They strolled past to the exit and Turdlet opened it in just a few seconds.

"This is it?" she asked.

"That's it," said Gassy.

Turkey wasn't after money. She didn't need it. What she wanted was unique items, the kind that made her stand out. The kind that garnered respect. There was easily more of that on the corpses in this room than the gnomes would ever have.

"I hope I never see you again," she announced before disappearing back into the pit.

* * * * *

The Hilltop Resort wasn't the most famous spot in Under-arraz (sigh), or the most creatively named. It had, however, very recently made a major change from a luxury destination to refugee shelter. Situated less than twenty minutes' walk from the little hovel our gnomes had recently visited, it was the perfect place for newly de-homed families to watch their beloved town crumble under the power of the uncontrollable fire. At this point, everyone was quite disappointed they hadn't invested more in magic but still not one local dared blame the ribbons.

Mothers, fathers, sons, and daughters all huddled together with a level of denial that rivalled that of a balding twenty-something. Those that had already accepted the destruction of everything they held dear were awash with ghostly expressions that seemed to suck the sounds from the rare jovial conversations around them. Even the animals finding refuge in the resort were somehow more sombre than usual. The sheep no longer bleated, instead employing far more of a blurt. Horses no longer whinnied; they preferred a defeated harrumph, not dissimilar to the sound of a grandfather who looked forward to bangers and mash for dinner only to find that today was vegetable stew day. The more fantastical creatures were less welcome in the town, other than as a meat to eat, so their displeasure was somewhat lesser than their unmagical counterparts.

With all this negativity and earth-shattering displeasure, there was none more out of place than the gnomes'. Borty, Gassy, and Turdlet sat on bar stools on a deck overlooking one of the steeper slopes the resort-shelter had to offer. There they watched the not-city burning.

"That was a shit-show," declared Borty.

"Things didn't quite go to plan," added Gassy.

"I thought it was fun." Not surprised, the others decided to avoid asking Turdlet to expand on his thoughts.

"What a waste of time," said Borty. "Just a little chump change, that's all we got."

"That and these," said Turdlet as he presented the missing pages from the Necrognomicon.

"I'm not surprised," said Gassy. "Don't act like this is some big reveal."

"Oh c'mon. Be a little surprised," said Turdlet.

"No."

"Those are the pages you used to stop me from dying!" said Borty.

"I figured they might come in handy. Cheaper than potions, anyway."

"That's a pretty good get. Even so, I'm sorry I brought you fellas into this," began Borty, "next time I'll check our reward will be from a legitimate sponsor."

"Kinda weird MagInc would sponsor the competition if they also sponsored Breezy to win," said Turdlet.

"They likely sponsored him to hedge their bets. They clearly wanted that book, bad. Maybe Breezy was just there to give competitors a reason to hand in the book and not take it for ourselves. I know that's pretty much how it worked for us." Gassy's reasoning seemed sound. Arguing over MagInc's motives wasn't going to get them anywhere. They agreed it wasn't their concern anymore.

"Let's just hope they have honest intentions," said Borty. As his comment clicked, the others slowly chuckled until their chuckles evolved into a hearty laugh. Their laughter became so disruptive that people around them looked on them with disgust and whispers.

Gassy suddenly perked up as he noticed a young woman sitting at the other end of the deck. Her darkened hair was ruffled, with its frayed edges completely burned. Lines of clear skin ran down her ash covered face where tears had long since dried. She stared out into the fire, open-mouthed and motionless.

"Hey!" yelled Gassy, "it's Josi."

"So it is," said Borty.

"I should probably say hi. Maybe she needs someone to console her."

"In no world would seeing your grim face be a comfort to anyone," said Turdlet.

"What the... Borty, say something," whined Gassy.

"It's up to you, bud," said Borty.

Gassy looked back to Josi. She hadn't budged. In her hands, she tightly squeezed an empty trifle glass.

"Yeah. I think I'll leave her be," said Gassy as his eyes wandered back to the fire.

The boys then sat in silence for a moment. They watched the last survivors slump in safety. They could all do with a nice long nap.

"Oh, I almost forgot," Gassy excitedly exclaimed. He quickly rummaged through his bag and whisked out his Crimicon t-shirt. With an ear-to-ear smile on his face, he shuffled it down his body. It was a tight fit, but it didn't matter.

"Very nice," said Borty.

"I didn't even get to use my emergency explosives," said Turdlet out of the blue.

"Maybe next time."

Epilogue

Mr Lawderman sat in a cornerless room so sterilised from colour that a droplet of sweat stood out like a daisy in dirt. He wasn't sitting on a chair, but a protrusion from the wall. It was very slightly uncomfortable. The kind of uncomfortable that just about stops you from falling asleep. Mr Lawderman was clasping the Necrognomicon firmly in both gloved hands as he looked forward. The room had a subtle hum coming from the lights above, lights that he could only assume were powered by essence.

There was one other person in the room. A fae. They sat, patiently waiting as Mr Lawderman was, holding a sword shimmering with a purple glow. This unique sword looked to have a bone hilt with a tiny skull on its pommel. Mr Lawderman was unfazed by the fae's presence, past anything more than a polite nod.

The time passed with no way of knowing how long it had been, but Mr Lawderman didn't dare complain. Neither the fae nor Mr Lawderman shuffled in their seats. The only emotion they expressed was joy when they heard the click of a door.

A woman, dressed in what can only be described as business attire, strutted out of the door like she *meant* business. Her hair was pinned back so tightly that it was difficult to tell which of the pair she was looking at.

"You now," she said. She didn't gesture or even glance at who she was referring to. She walked back through the door leaving the fae and Mr Lawderman to have a silent discussion as to who should go. The consensus was Mr Lawderman, he *was* there first. He hurried to his feet and rushed to keep up with the businesswoman, while making as little noise as possible.

After a short walk, the woman stood before a glass door and turned back to Mr Lawderman with a cold stare and her hand held out.

"The book," she said.

"Oh yes, of course," Mr Lawderman handed her the book, doing his best not to wince as she grabbed it with her bare hand. She slid the glass door open and strutted in. Mr Lawderman cautiously followed as he inspected the new room.

The space was enormous. On his left and right side was open space across a flat metallic floor stopping at two towering cloudy glass gates on either side. The only notable feature in this untarnished room was a desk at its end, the same desk the woman and the Necrognomicon powered towards. Behind the desk read the words 'MagInc'.

"Come closer, Mr Lawderman." A voice echoed from the desk. The man behind the woman got to his feet with a smile on his face. He was wearing a carefully cropped suit out of a material so refined you could smell the manufacturing processes. He edged around to the front of the table, gesturing Mr Lawderman forward.

"Sir," said the woman, handing him the book before stepping to one side.

"Thank you, Ms Pell." The man, a seemingly ordinary human, inspected the book as Ms Pell disappeared from Mr Lawderman's view. "Mr Lawderman. It seems you've put our puzzle pieces to good use."

"Yes sir. Everything went according to plan, mostly." Mr Lawderman lowered his head as he caught a sharp glance from the man.

"And when you say mostly, what are you referring to?"

"There are a few pages missing. I've a feeling the gnomes who handed it in might be to blame for their disappearance."

"That was to be expected. No matter. We shan't concern ourselves with it, shall we Mr Lawderman?" the man's squinting smile felt like a child's attempt to mimic adult behaviour. It was close to normal, but something was off.

"Of course, sir. We shouldn't worry. Although, we did also lose Under-arraz," Mr Lawderman paused to sigh before realising he didn't need to anymore. Nobody would kill him for it here.

"You're referring to the fire. Yes, we had expected that, but it was a few months earlier than planned. Again, no matter, the puzzle pieces will find their way back into circulation. They always do." The man circled back around his metallic desk and settled in an uncomfortable looking chair. Even sitting down, he was taller than Mr Lawderman.

"So what will you do now that you've acquired the Necrognom—"

"What about the target? Tell me how that went."

"The target, sir?" Mr Lawderman glanced at the book now resting on the desk. He didn't want to point out the obvious.

"Yes, Day Lord, or whatever he calls himself these days."

"Oh," Mr Lawderman frowned, "we unfortunately lost him. I hear he was killed shortly before his manor exploded."

"Good," said the man.

"Sir?"

"He shan't be missed. The upper council won't dilly-dally. No doubt, they will soon be holding elections for Day Lord's replacement." The man unbuttoned his jacket and carefully hung it up in a hidden closet behind him, right underneath the letter 'g' in 'MagInc'. In place, he donned a rather ragged red traditional robe. His face didn't bother hiding his disgust.

"That's a lower council robe," said Mr Lawderman. His statement was closer to a question than certainty.

"Good eye, Mr Lawderman." He paused as he adjusted his collar and sleeves. "I've got something I'd like to show those good eyes of yours, Mr Lawderman."

The man walked to one of the glass gates nearby, standing beside it in expectation. Mr Lawderman hurried behind him with faint excitement. The glass slid open. Mr Lawderman hobbled onto an unending platform with the bottom of his jaw dragging behind him.

"This is—" he began, unsure how to continue. "What is this?"

The room was filled with floating glass tubes, vials, containers, display cases, and more. Inside was damn near everything. Jewellery, swords, bows, amour, trinkets, food. There was a piece of everything.

"What do you think it is, Mr Lawderman?"

"Wait a minute. That's the Amulet of Aimlessness!" Mr Lawderman pointed to a contained amulet floating around the room without much direction. "And that, over there, it's the Armour of Amore," he continued pointing at a heart-shaped breastplate. The listing continued, each one he pointed at brought him that much closer to ecstasy. This was his wildest dream. "You've got half the magical items I've dreamed of seeing."

The man winced at Mr Lawderman's joy, "Your knowledge of the old-world essence is impressive, Mr

Lawderman. These enchantments were the source of power for people all across the country. Of course, most don't mean much in the way of our new essence weapons. No, there's only one artefact that matters now." The man walked ahead of Mr Lawderman on the platform, admiring his own work.

"The Necrognomicon?" said Mr Lawderman, knowing full well that half the things he'd listed off were ten-times more powerful.

The man laughed, if it could be called a laugh. It sounded more like a stray dog trying to dislodge a piece of bone stuck in the back of its throat.

"No, Mr Lawderman. Not the Necrognomicon." The man pointed down, below the platform. "That."

Stretching out further than Mr Lawderman had ever walked in his life, a huge golden puzzle lay sprawled in pieces. Gronks of varying sizes busied around the puzzle, slotting pieces where they belonged with a little cheer for every successful pairing.

"The puzzle. You're trying to build it."

"Well, that one was quite obvious." The man smiled with his mouth, but not his eyes. He just stared at Mr Lawderman with his fake smile.

"But you'd need every piece to finish it. You'd bankrupt everyone in the country!"

"In a way, yes. But we'll introduce a new currency. Eventually. Out with the old and in with the new, as they say."

Mr Lawderman started to back away.

"What's the matter Mr Lawderman? Am I boring you?" asked the man.

"No sir, not at all." Mr Lawderman raised his hands. "I just really ought to be going. Business to do, that's all."

"And what business would that be?" The man presented another eerie smile. He began to don some white and red gloves. "We hired your services exclusively, isn't that right?"

Mr Lawderman hesitated. "Well, yes sir. But... I still have work to do."

"Is that so, Mr Lawderman? I was under the impression this was our last assignment for you. Am I wrong, Ms Pell?"

"No, sir." Ms Pell was standing right behind Mr Lawderman. He didn't even hear her approach.

"There's plenty I can do for—"

"Ms Pell, if you would," said the man. Out of nowhere, Ms Pell grabbed Mr Lawderman by the collar and launched him over the railings and down onto the puzzle below. His face cracked inside itself and the gronks didn't even flinch. "Damn good throw, Ms Pell."

"Thank you, sir."

"I've an election to attend. Keep things on course while I'm gone, Ms Pell."

"Yes, Mr Future."

Thank You

for reading the first instalment of Game of Gnomes:
Game of Gnomes: The Necrognomicon

We hope you enjoyed it.

Who made this book?
Critical Tales are a small publishing company based in
Shrewsbury, U.K. It's made up of a group of aspiring and
creative individuals looking to bring fresh and uplifting
material to people like you.

By purchasing and reading this book you're helping us to
create more!

If you enjoyed the book then leave a review on your favourite
platform or head over to our socials and
tell us directly.

www.criticaltales.co.uk
@criticaltalesofficial